KALPAR
HOW THE ALIENS WERE WON

HONEY PHILLIPS

Copyright © 2024 by Honey Phillips

All rights reserved. No part of this book may be used or reproduced by any means, graphic, electronic, or mechanical, including photocopying, recording, taping or by any information storage retrieval system without the written permission of the author.

Disclaimer

This book is a work of fiction. Names, characters, places, and incidents are products of the author's imagination or are used fictitiously and are not to be construed as real. Any resemblance to actual events, locales, organizations, or people, living or dead, is entirely coincidental.

Cover Design by Mariah Sinclair
Edited by Lindsay York at LY Publishing Services

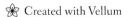 Created with Vellum

CHAPTER 1

Constance looked at herself in the mirror and bit back a sigh.

"It's very... grand," she managed.

"Only the finest materials were used, as per your father's specifications," Adele said severely. The designer, a tall, thin woman clad in an exquisitely tailored black dress, looked down her nose at Constance and allowed herself a discreet cough. "Perhaps a little makeup might be appropriate."

This time the sigh did escape. The deep purple satin, heavily embroidered with gold thread, only made her already pale coloring look even more washed out, but her father had decreed that purple and gold were his House colors and ordered that her dress for the ball reflect those colors. Humans did not actually have Houses, but that hadn't stopped her father. He'd decided he liked the sound of it and declared that they were now House Thompson.

He'll be calling himself Lord Thompson next, she thought bitterly as she took another look hoping that the dress might improve at second glance. It didn't.

The collar of the outer robe rose up behind her head to form a stiff, rounded peak, making it almost impossible to turn her head without risking injury, then fell stiffly to the ground. The stiff fabric did nothing to flatter her small breasts or her slender figure. The high neck and long sleeves of the gold satin under robe shrouded even more of her body.

Since her father never allowed her to wear anything that was remotely revealing in public, he would no doubt be extremely pleased. The only part of her that was actually visible was the pale oval of her face—even her hands were covered by the oversized flounces at the end of the long tight sleeves, making it almost impossible to touch anyone with her bare skin.

"Perhaps," she agreed, even though she had no intention of painting herself up like a doll for her father's pleasure. "Do you need to make any more adjustments?"

She hoped that Adele might decide to loosen the high, tight collar, but the other woman only shook her head.

"Not unless your father requests any additional changes."

Adele didn't ask if Constance wanted any changes, but then she didn't expect her to. The seamstress's eyes flicked towards the door at the back of the room that led to the hallway, where Constance's guards waited. They were technically outside the large dressing room, but only a curtain covered the entrance.

"Would you like me to help you change?"

"Yes, please. I'm pretty sure I can't get out of this dress by myself," she said dryly.

Adele unfastened the complicated series of ribbons that held the outer robe together, then stripped off the purple monstrosity, and Constance breathed a sigh of relief. Because of the amount of gold thread, the robe weighed a ton. The seamstress untied the additional ribbons down the back of the gold satin underdress, and then she was free.

She pulled her own dress over her head. Although it also had a high neck and long sleeves, the simple white sheath was made from a light cotton that floated gently around her ankles. Her unruly hair had escaped its braid again so she tied it back into a quick knot before turning to thank Adele. It wasn't the other woman's fault that the dress was so unflattering—she had no doubt followed her father's instructions—and the workmanship was exquisite.

"I can take the dress with me," she offered, but Adele looked scandalized by the idea.

"The garment must be carefully packed for transit. I will bring it with me on the night of the ball."

Transit? They were less than a mile from Thompson Tower. But she didn't argue with that either. Instead, she smiled politely, nodded again, and left the room. In the hallway, Oxmar, one of her guards, was looming over Adele's assistant Carol. He probably thought he was flirting but the girl only looked terrified.

"Adele is waiting for you, Carol," she said calmly.

The girl gave her a grateful look and hurried past her into the work room. Oxmar scowled at her, but she ignored him. He might have been crude and obnoxious, but he was too afraid of her father to cause her any real trouble. Rogut, her other guard, was another matter. Although he too was afraid of her father, he was both brutal and vicious and she prayed she would never find herself alone with him.

"About fucking time," Rogut muttered, just loud enough for her to hear.

Ignoring him as well, she passed through the small reception area and the locked doors that separated the workroom from the rest of the store. Her father expected his staff to keep his daughter confined when she came for her fittings. It might have made more sense to have her dress fitted in the tower, but her father enjoyed forcing the designers to accommodate his unreasonable demands.

Although it was already well past normal business hours, several customers still lingered in the elegant boutique. Two women glanced in their direction, their mouths tightening as they recognized her, while the men who must have accompanied them stared at her with more than passing interest.

Oxmar glared at the men, who immediately looked away, but not before Constance caught the speculation in their expressions. She couldn't blame them—her father dangled her in front of the most powerful males in the city like an expensive jewel. Only the fact that he enjoyed the game—and had yet to identify a suitor who had sufficient wealth and influence to tempt him— had kept her unmarried so far.

Not that marriage was necessarily his end goal. Under the right circumstances she had no doubt he would just as happily sell her as a high-priced concubine. *At least that would put a more honest face on the transaction*, she thought bitterly as she donned her cloak and swept by the other customers, keeping her head high.

The breeze from the ocean whipped strands of blonde hair across her face, chilly after the heat of the day, and she pulled her cloak more closely around her. The street bustled with activity as the surrounding merchants closed their shops and people embarked on their evening activities. She caught the mouthwatering aroma of spiced meat pies drifting from a nearby food stall and her stomach rumbled. When was the last time she'd had the chance to sample such simple pleasures?

Not since Algar, her last bodyguard, had disappeared. He'd been as big and brutish as her present bodyguards, but his appearance had been deceptive. A kind heart lurked beneath that rough exterior. He'd taken pity on her restricted existence and occasionally allowed her to indulge in such harmless behaviors as visiting the market. Unfortunately, he had paid for that kindness when her father had discovered her activities. She hadn't seen him since.

The reminder caused a sudden surge of rebellion.

"I want to go this way," she said, turning down the street towards the market square.

"Your father instructed us to return directly to the tower," Oxmar rumbled, lumbering after her.

She saw the guards exchange a look when she didn't obey, but she ignored them both, picking up her pace as the lively sounds and smells of the open-air market grew stronger. The square opened up before them, a kaleidoscope of vibrant colors and bustling activity. Vendors hawked their wares from rickety stalls, calling out enticingly to the throngs of people passing by.

A beggar woman held an infant to her breast, rattling a chipped cup at those who strode past. Her heart ached for the two of them, but she still felt a pang of jealousy at the tender way the woman was cradling her child. Her mother had died when she was very young, and she had only the vaguest memories of her.

"You there! Sweet cakes to tempt a lovely lady!"

She turned towards the jovial call. A plump matron waved a tray piled high with fried dough dusted with sugar. Her mouth watered, but despite her father's wealth, she was never permitted to carry any credits of her own. Algar would have bought the treat for her, but she knew better than to ask Oxmar or Rogut. She gave the woman an apologetic smile and moved on.

The glint of torchlight on metal caught her eye, drawing her attention to a weathered old male peddling curious trinkets. Baubles, amulets, and talismans of all kinds adorned his makeshift stall, but one in particular snagged her gaze—a tarnished medallion dangling from a frayed cord. There was nothing remarkable about it except the detailed markings etched into its surface, and she traced the faded lines, curious about their meaning.

"Ah, I see you've an eye for the unusual." The vendor's gravelly voice startled her and she turned to see him giving her an appraising look. "That there's a freedom talisman from the Korlian Rift. It's imbued with the wanderlust of thousands of nomads searching for a future."

She gave him a startled look as she ran her fingers over the markings again.

"Does it really grant freedom?"

Although she tried to sound skeptical, even she could hear the longing in her voice.

"Freedom is a journey, not a destination." He tapped the talisman. "This is but the first step."

Rogut's harsh grip closed on her wrist, his meaty fingers digging into the fragile bones.

"Enough. Back to the tower. Now."

"How dare you touch me?" she said furiously. "Let go of me at once."

Malevolence gleamed in his eyes as he looked down at her, and her heart started to pound. They both knew there was no way she could escape that cruel grip unless he chose to let her go. Then Oxmar gave him an uneasy look and tugged on his arm.

"Better let her go. Her father wouldn't like it," he warned.

Rogut stared at her a moment longer, his fingers tightening, but then he shrugged and released her.

"Tower. Now."

Knowing that her small attempt at rebellion was over, she gave a quick nod. As she turned to accompany them, the vendor slipped the talisman into her palm.

"I'm sorry, but I can't take this," she said quickly. "I don't have any credits."

He shook his head and closed her fingers over the worn metal.

"It's a gift, child. Perhaps it will be the first step you need."

He turned away before she could thank him and Rogut gave her a threatening look. Lifting her chin with as much dignity as possible, she tucked the talisman in her pocket and followed him.

CHAPTER 2

Constance sat silently in the back of the luxurious hover vehicle as they returned to the sleek obsidian spire of Thompson Tower. Her guards rode with the driver during the trip, but they rejoined her as soon as she stepped out of the vehicle. After undergoing the usual security scans, they ascended rapidly in the private elevator. She could feel Rogut's gaze on her back for the entire trip, and the knowledge sent a chill down her spine. If he had grown bold enough to touch her —to hurt her—how much further would he go?

Oxmar was right—her father would not like the fact that the guard had touched her—but he would be just as displeased that she had visited the market. He might even consider Rogut's actions justifiable punishment. She was still considering her options when the elevator reached the lobby leading to the first floor of the penthouse. Even the lobby was designed to showcase her father's wealth with inlaid marble floors and a glittering chandelier below what appeared to be a glass roof showing the night sky. It was an illusion, of course—a cleverly programmed artificial view.

The ornate double doors on the far side of the lobby swung open as she approached. The guards waited for her to pass through them before they crossed to the smaller door leading to the security office and their quarters. The double doors swung shut behind her with the soft thud of a prison door as a waiting attendant hurried forward to take her cloak.

"Your father wishes to see you, Miss Thompson. He is in the small receiving room."

"Very well. I'll join him there."

She tried to keep her steps from lagging as she made her way through the maze of corridors, ignoring her surroundings. Polished marble floors gleamed beneath her feet and priceless artwork covered the walls, but the whole effect was cold and unwelcoming, more like a museum than a home.

Small was, of course, relative. The small receiving room was actually a spacious room with a high ceiling and gilt-encrusted walls. As usual, her father was seated in a high-back chair positioned squarely before the floor-to-ceiling windows that offered a panoramic view over Port Cantor. He was impeccably dressed in an exquisitely tailored suit, every platinum hair in place.

"You wished to see me, Father?" she said, keeping her tone carefully neutral as she crossed to stand before him.

After a brief but significant pause, he raised his head from the datapad he was studying and surveyed her. Those cold blue eyes, so like her own yet completely lacking in warmth, appraised her from head to toe as if searching for any hint of defiance or disobedience. She fought the urge to fidget under that penetrating scrutiny.

"I believe I have secured an appropriate match for you," he said without preamble. "Lord Vexian of the Kalron Clan. It could be an advantageous connection."

Lord Vexian? He was almost as old as her father and his reputation was just as unsavory. If what she'd heard was true, he'd come to Port Cantor because he was no longer welcome on his own planet but he'd brought a good deal of wealth with him and accumulated more since his arrival. Her heart pounded as she tried to think of some argument to convince her father that the marriage was not a good idea, although she knew that his only interest in any potential spouse was as a business transaction to further his interests.

"Surely you don't expect me to enter into an arranged marriage with someone I've never met?" she asked desperately. "We don't even know each other, let alone love each other."

A muscle ticked in his jaw and she knew she'd overstepped, but to her surprise he didn't rebuke her outright.

"Love is a weakness, an indulgence for lesser beings," he said coldly. "Lord Vexian simply desires an untouched, attractive, well-bred female to act as his wife and hostess, and he is prepared to pay handsomely for that privilege."

"An undamaged product," she muttered. "One who has not been used and discarded by previous owners."

"That is not amusing, Constance. You should be grateful that I have been so vigilant about preserving your value. As a result, you will be in a position of wealth and status."

And just as trapped as she was now.

"Or would you prefer wandering aimlessly through the marketplace, your time wasted on pointless pursuits?" His lips tightened. "Perhaps you even enjoyed being manhandled by your bodyguard today."

Why was she even surprised that he knew about the illicit visit? At least he seemed annoyed by Rogut's behavior—perhaps even annoyed enough to find her another bodyguard. His next words confirmed it.

"Since we are at a delicate point in our negotiations, I have taken additional steps to ensure that there are no last minute changes in your... status. This is Kalpar. He will be your new bodyguard."

A huge male suddenly stepped out of a corner of the room and she jumped. He had been standing so quietly and she had been so focused on her father that she hadn't noticed him until he moved. *How could I have missed him?*

He was tall, at least a head taller than either Oxmar or Rogut, but built on leaner lines. His skin was a pale lavender, like light reflecting off the edge of a well-honed blade. His hair was a much darker shade of purple, and for a hysterical moment she wondered if her father had chosen him because he matched the House colors.

His features were more angular than human, but they would have been attractive if they hadn't been locked into such a cold expression. His eyes were a shade of silver so pale they were almost white. As their eyes met, it suddenly felt as if all the air had been sucked out of the room, and it took far too long before she could force herself to look away. As she did, she noticed the deadly-looking knives attached to his belt and a chill ran down her spine.

"Kalpar will remain with you continuously from now until the negotiations are complete."

He couldn't possibly mean that, could he? The prospect of her already severely limited freedom disappearing completely made her heart flutter frantically.

"Continuously? You don't mean—"

"Continuously," her father said firmly. "Night and day. Kalpar is a Catari," he added meaningfully, and she gave him a confused look.

"Which means I have no interest in any female except my chosen mate."

Kalpar's cold voice should have added to her panic, but for some reason she found the deep voice unexpectedly reassuring.

"I'm sure that's very nice, but I really don't need a twenty-four—"

"Continuously."

Her father picked up his datapad again, clearly dismissing her. Long years of experience had taught her the futility of arguing with any of his decisions. She turned towards the door, almost as reluctant to leave as she'd been to enter. Kalpar fell into step behind her, moving so silently that she wouldn't have known he'd moved at all if she hadn't been looking right at him. It took every ounce of self-control not to shiver as his presence enveloped her like an icy shroud.

As soon as they were clear of the door, she gathered her courage and looked up at her new guard. The same emotionless eyes she had encountered earlier looked down at her—and kept looking. Despite his words to her father, the intensity in his gaze suddenly made her wonder if he was as uninterested in women as her father had claimed.

Forcing herself to look away from that intense expression, she headed for the internal elevators. He followed without a word.

"Are you always this quiet?" she finally demanded as they reached them.

A raised eyebrow was his only response.

The elevators were located in the center of the tower. The three banks of elevators in the outer lobby provided access to the lower floors, including the garage and the maintenance area, the other offices and the rooms which housed various live-in staff. One of the small elevators ahead of them only went to their private quarters, while the other went straight to the elaborately landscaped roof. Her father liked entertaining up there—the fact that the area was higher than all of the surrounding buildings a clear testament to his power.

As they reached the elevator, Kalpar reached past her to press the call button and then remained at her side. Very close to her side.

His muscular arm brushed against her shoulder and his cool breath feathered across her face as he stared down at her with those emotionless eyes again. Other than at the formal dances her father forced her to attend, it had been years since she'd been this close to a man—and even then only a handful of men were ever allowed near her—and her body immediately reacted to his presence. Heat flooded through her, chasing the chill from her bones, and she could feel a traitorous blush start to creep up her cheeks.

"May I have some space please?"

He raised an eyebrow again, then took a single step back. It didn't help—she could still feel his presence surrounding her. When the elevator arrived, he ushered her inside then pressed his thumb on the reader. Her heart sank as the doors immediately closed. Her father had given him direct access to their private quarters. She stared straight ahead as they climbed quickly to the next floor, but she was all too aware of that massive body only inches away.

When the doors slid open again, she hurried out into the main hall of the penthouse. This area was as elaborately decorated as the floor below, even though very few people other than she and her father were ever allowed this far, but it was just as soulless.

As she headed towards the west wing where her suite was located, he stayed just behind her, close enough that she could feel the heat emanating from his body. In the past she had always found the silence that followed her bodyguards' departure comforting, but the more time she spent in his silent presence the less comfortable she felt. She would have even welcomed a crude comment from Rogut by now, anything to break the heavy weight of his presence.

When they reached the door to her suite, he opened it and waited for her to precede him before following her into the sitting room. Ignoring him as best she could, she crossed over to her bedroom door, only to find him right behind her again as she stepped through it.

"What do you think you're doing?"

Her voice threatened to tremble as she looked up at that impassive face, but he gave no sign that he was aware of her discomfort.

"I am assuming my position."

"Your position?"

"Where you go, I go."

"I'm sure that my father didn't mean actually in my bedroom."

He folded his arms across his chest and raised that damn eyebrow again.

"I will be at your side at all times. When you eat, when you sleep, when you bathe. If you wish me to turn my back at certain moments, I shall. But I will be there."

She had intended to take a long hot bath, but the prospect of doing so with him in the room was too unnerving to contemplate. Instead, she wandered out onto the balcony that ran along one side of her rooms. It appeared to be open to the air, but like so much of her life, it was an illusion. She pressed her hand against the bulletproof glass enclosing it and stared out into the night.

Perhaps it was just as well the balcony was enclosed—at the current moment flinging herself off of it seemed like a more desirable alternative than passing from her father's control into that of another ruthless male, one who didn't even have the shallow tie of blood to restrain his behavior. A tear trickled down her cheek, but she refused to give in to despair.

Instead, she put her hand in her pocket and closed her fingers around the worn metal of the talisman. The vendor had said it was the first step on the journey to freedom. Now all she had to do was to find the next step.

CHAPTER 3

Kalpar watched his new charge as she stood out on the balcony staring out into the distance, an unwilling flicker of compassion stirring at the sight of her hunched posture and despairing attitude. She was nothing like he'd expected. He'd assumed Marshall's daughter would be a spoiled, arrogant female—the feminine counterpart of her father. Instead, she was small and shy, with an air of fragility which called to his almost forgotten protective instincts.

Her delicate beauty didn't help. He knew human females could be attractive—several of the former warriors from his squad had found human mates—but he'd never encountered anyone as lovely as this little human. Several silvery blonde curls had escaped the knot at the nape of her neck, framing her delicate features. Her soft pale skin made it easy for him to watch the rapid beat of the pulse at the base of her neck, and his mouth watered. It would be so easy to sink his fangs into that tempting little spot.

His fangs? The thought shocked him. A Catari's fangs never emerged unless he was in a mating frenzy and Kalpar had long since accepted that there would be no mate in his future. *It is merely an assertion of dominance*, he assured himself.

As if sensing the danger she faced, she shivered and then returned to the sitting room. Despite her small size she moved with a surprising grace, her white dress drifting around her slender body as she paced from one end of the spacious room to the other. As he leaned against the wall and watched her, he found himself wondering about the body beneath the voluminous gown. With those small breasts and slender hips, he doubted that she had many curves, but at the same time there was an indefinable something about her that suggested a hidden sensuality.

And her father thought Lord Vexian was the appropriate male to awaken that sensuality? The thought disturbed him far more than it should. Although he had never encountered the other male, his reputation was well known in Port Cantor. Unlike Marshall Thompson, Vexian made little effort to conceal his illicit activities, relying on bribery and threats to avoid the law. Kalpar hated the thought of this delicate female in Vexian's brutish hands.

It is not my concern, he reminded himself. He was here for one purpose only—to find out why Marshall Thompson was so interested in the land he and his fellow warriors owned. Their land consisted of a small cluster of previously abandoned farms that they were in the process of rehabilitating. The property was located a considerable distance from Port Cantor, and it possessed no intrinsic value of which they were aware. They weren't even close enough to the coast, let alone any larger settlements, to be useful for storing stolen goods.

And yet Marshall had made at least two previous attempts to infiltrate and survey the farm. He was clearly searching for something, but they had no idea what. Kalpar had made it his mission to find out, even if that meant using Marshall's daughter as a pawn. No matter how distasteful the idea seemed currently, protecting his fellow warriors was more important than this frail human.

The sight of her distress still bothered him, and he found himself speaking.

"Have you eaten?"

"What?"

She gave him a startled look, as if the idea of food were strange to her. Perhaps her body was so fragile because she didn't pay attention to such things. That at least he could remedy. He strode over to the communication panel and ordered a light meal to be delivered.

"I'm really not hungry," she protested, but he ignored her. He had accepted the responsibility for her wellbeing, even for the short time he expected to be a member of the household, and his future plans didn't change that responsibility.

His position as her bodyguard had been an unexpected stroke of luck. One of his contacts had arranged to have him interviewed for a position as a household guard. However, when he'd come to apply, Warshan, the chief of Marshall's security forces, had given him an appraising look.

"Is it true that a Catari male is incapable of being aroused by anyone other than his mate?"

There was a slight sneer behind the question, but he ignored it and nodded. It actually wasn't entirely true—there was a brief period during a male's adolescence when his body could experience arousal. Like most Catari males he had taken advantage of that time, but he had found it neither pleasurable nor rewarding. As soon as he reached full adulthood, even such unsatisfactory attempts were no longer possible. Since that was also the time at which he decided to leave his home planet and join the Alliance forces, he had known there would be no mate in his future. He had considered the sacrifice worthwhile in order to escape.

Shaking off the unpleasant memories, he went to answer a discreet knock on the door. A young serving maid stood outside with a tray, giving him a wide-eyed look. He took the tray from her trembling hands and dismissed her, ignoring her ineffectual attempt to protest.

After placing the tray on a small table near the windows, he checked the contents. A bowl containing colorful cubes of fruit, an assortment of cheeses and thinly sliced meats, and a selection of small sweet cakes, plus a pitcher containing an effervescent but non-alcoholic liquid, all beautifully prepared and arranged. Next time he would specify a hot dish as well, but it would do.

"Eat," he ordered.

"I told you I'm not hungry," she said defiantly, but then her stomach rumbled.

"Your body betrays you. Do you think that refusing to eat is a reasonable way of defying your father? Or me? I fail to see the logic in making yourself weaker when you are already so frail."

Her small chin rose at that and she glared at him. He found her defiance unexpectedly pleasurable. Her father had not succeeded in completely crushing her spirit.

When she continued to look at him defiantly, he strode over to pick up one of the cubes of fruit and held it out to her.

"Open. Now."

"That's ridiculous! You don't expect me to let you feed me, do you?"

"If necessary."

He could see her wavering as the scent of the fruit drifted to her nose, but he was sure her refusal had more to do with stubborn pride than lack of hunger.

"Eat, Constance."

When he traced the cube over her pretty mouth, hunger won out and she accepted it, wrapping her soft little lips around the cube. Her mouth brushed against his fingers in the process, sending an unfamiliar jolt of sensation through his body. Frowning at the unexpected reaction, he took a step back and gestured at the tray again.

"Now eat. Unless you wish me to feed you the rest?"

To his surprise, she gave him an unreadable look and then obeyed, seating herself gracefully in the chair next to the table. Instead of proceeding, she toyed with her fork for a moment, avoiding his gaze.

"Do you want to join me?" she asked hesitantly.

He raised an eyebrow.

"I doubt your father would approve," he said dryly.

Her shoulders sagged, but then she lifted her chin and gave him that same defiant look.

"So?"

He hid a smile as he shrugged and joined her, ignoring the faint color in her cheeks. He did enjoy her spirit, but his enjoyment was irrelevant. He was here for information and nothing else.

Once she had started eating, it was clear that she was in fact hungry. He surreptitiously checked to be sure she was eating enough, confining himself to sipping on the sparkling juice.

After she had finished, she nibbled at one of the sweet cakes, closing her eyes and making soft little sounds of pleasure as she savored the taste. Those same soft sounds threatened his iron control as she licked crumbs from her fingers, but he successfully ignored her sensual enjoyment. When she had finished, he gave her a stern look.

"Do you intend to bathe before retiring?"

"Bathe? What… what does that have to do with you?"

Her cheeks flushed a delicious shade of pink as she reached for her juice, and he allowed himself to show his amusement at her discomfort.

"Just determining our next step."

"Our next step?"

He raised an eyebrow.

"I told you I would be with you night and day."

"That doesn't mean you have to be in the bathroom while I bathe!" she exclaimed.

"When you eat, when you bathe, when you sleep—you are either by my side or you are in my sight."

"But..."

Her shoulders sagged again as she stared at his implacable face.

"Fine," she muttered, then rose and led the way into her bedroom and across it to the bathing room, hesitating at the doorway. "Look, you can see there isn't any other way into the room. I'm sure it would be fine if you waited outside."

"There is a window."

He gestured at the large arched window behind the gently steaming bathing pool and she gave him a skeptical look.

"We're hundreds of feet in the air—who could come through there?"

"It is a possibility for a determined intruder." He shrugged. "As is the ventilation system and possibly the plumbing conduits."

"You have got to be kidding me." She marched into the room, stopping again when he followed. "No."

"Yes. You may undress and prepare for your bath while I stand with my back to you, but I will remain in the room."

"Oh my God!"

She stomped her foot in a surprisingly adorable display of frustration, and he hid a smile as he turned his back and waited for her to comply. After a few seconds of heavy breathing, she sighed and he heard rustling behind him as she apparently gave up the fight.

Although he kept his back turned, he focused on every sound, imagining her removing her dress and uncovering her slender body. Would her pale skin flush as she stepped into the hot water? For a male who prided himself on his discipline, the urge to turn around and watch her bathe was surprisingly powerful but he maintained his position.

Water splashed softly as she lowered herself into the tub, and her scent filled the room. Not the heavy floral scent he would have associated with a pampered, privileged female but a fresh, clean scent that he found unexpectedly appealing. *Fuck. Everything about her was appealing. And irrelevant*, he reminded himself. He had a mission to complete.

That didn't stop awareness from prickling his skin as he continued to wait with his back to her, and when he heard her climb out of the tub, he could all too clearly envision the water streaming down her naked body. That unfamiliar sensation washed over him again as he listened to her movements. He clamped down ruthlessly on the impulse to turn around, waiting instead for her to tell him she was ready.

"I'm dressed," she said, her voice a little unsteady, and he turned.

As he'd expected, her pale skin was flushed from the heat of the bath. The white cotton of her nightgown clung slightly to her damp body. Although it too covered most of her body, it was much thinner and more revealing than her previous dress. He could see the slight curve of her waist and the stiff peaks of her nipples beneath the thin fabric. His fingers actually twitched with the urge to touch those tempting little buds.

Ignoring her disconcerted expression as well as his own impulses, he opened the bathroom door and motioned to the bed.

"Sleep."

"W-where are you going to sleep? And when, for that matter?"

He shrugged.

"I will get some rest while you sleep. The war taught me to be on guard even then." He slept so lightly that even the faintest sound would rouse him from his slumber. He couldn't remember the last time he'd passed an uninterrupted night. "As for where..."

He let the words linger as he glanced back at the bed and her breathing sped up, amused at her discomfort. But then he noticed that her nipples had stiffened even more and his amusement vanished as he fought a sudden urge to cup her small breasts and tease the erect tips. *What the fuck is wrong with me?* His inability to become aroused didn't prevent him from noticing an attractive female, but he rarely envisioned touching one.

"The chair by the window will suffice. It looks... comfortable," he added, managing to sound ironic. The plush chair was undoubtedly comfortable for a human, but his body was far too big for it.

"You would have more room on the sofa in the living area."

She gave him a hopeful look, but he shook his head.

"At my side or in my sight," he reminded her. "Now sleep."

She sighed, but went over to the bed and slipped beneath the covers, looking ridiculously small in the huge canopied bed. The bed didn't suit her, but then neither did the rest of the room. The furniture was too ornate and the expensive embroidered fabric that covered everything from the bed curtains to the upholstery was luxurious but uncomfortably stiff to the touch.

He suspected that the only actual sign of her personality was the small collection of books on the shelves next to the fireplace. He was tempted to explore them, but she had pulled the sheets up high enough so that only her eyes were visible, peeping uncertainly over the sheets. Instead, he ordered the lights off as he walked over to the chair he'd chosen. His night vision was excellent but unnecessary since the glow of city lights prevented the room from being in complete darkness.

"Do you want the curtains closed?"

"No. I like to be able to see the sky."

Her voice was soft and slightly breathless.

"Then go to sleep."

He sat down in the uncomfortable chair and put his legs up on a small ottoman. It only minimally improved the situation, but it was still a hundred times better than most of his nights during the war. He stretched and rolled his shoulders a couple of times, watching surreptitiously as her eyes widened at the movement. Her appreciative look was a little too satisfying and he forced himself to ignore it as he settled back in the chair.

Closing his eyes, he began the breathing exercises that would enable him to relax while still maintaining awareness. Before long he heard her breathing even out, but it was a long time before he fell asleep.

CHAPTER 4

Constance awoke with a start, her heart pounding and her skin flushed. The vivid dream still clung to her mind—Kalpar leaning over her, his silver eyes blazing as he watched her with an intensity that made her shiver. And he hadn't just been watching her—his hands had been caressing her, playing with her breasts and sliding down between her legs.

She squeezed her eyes shut, trying to will the inappropriate images away, but excitement still hummed through her veins. Her breasts ached and heat pulsed low in her stomach. She pressed her hands against her breasts in a vain attempt to suppress the ache but the pressure only increased her arousal. She peeped over at Kalpar, but his eyes were closed, his big body completely still.

Giving in to a reckless impulse, she tugged lightly at her nipples, almost gasping at the resulting rush of desire. She had touched herself before, but it had never felt this intense. Still keeping an eye on Kalpar, she slid one hand down under the sheet, pressing her thighs together against the demanding throb that greeted her touch.

Taking a deep breath, she tugged her nightgown up above her waist, then stoked her hand down across her quivering stomach to her bare mound. She shuddered as her middle finger slid further down and came into contact with the slickness her dream had caused.

She tried to keep her movements quiet and controlled as she circled her opening, but her breath caught anyway as she grazed over her swollen clit. As she circled it, her other hand tightened on her nipple, harder than she'd ever touched herself before but the pressure only added to her excitement. Her arousal grew until it was almost painful and she knew she was close, so close...

Kalpar's eyes flew open, blazing white in the dark room, just as her climax crashed down over her.

"Fuck," he growled.

She was still shuddering from her release as he dropped his feet to the floor and rose. He stalked towards the bed, his eyes focused on the hand that was still beneath the covers and felt her clit pulse with excitement.

"I wasn't... I just needed..."

The words stuck in her throat. She couldn't lie and say she hadn't been touching herself, not when the evidence was so damning.

He reached the bed, towering over her, his chest rising and falling with his heavy breathing, but she didn't flinch away from him. Instead, her heartbeat accelerated in anticipation.

He hesitated for a moment, his nostrils flaring, and then he yanked the sheet away.

That burning white gaze swept down over her exposed lower body, to her hand still buried between her legs.

"Look at you," he rasped. "So ripe for breeding. By now you would have been mated, safe in a house of your own."

"It was never an option," she whispered, remembering her father's cold determination to control her and keep her unsullied.

"I suppose not."

He bent down and she thought he was going to touch her, her heart hammering with excitement. Instead, he pulled the sheet back up over her body.

"I cannot give you what you so clearly need, so for both our sakes, I would appreciate it if you restrained yourself."

Anger vied with embarrassment and won out. She glared up at him.

"If you insist on remaining at my side, then you should be prepared for the consequences."

"You don't lack courage, do you, little human?" To her surprise, he actually sounded amused. "I find that I admire your defiance, but I still expect you to acquiesce to my request. There are several hours until dawn. Go back to sleep, Constance."

Ignoring her shock, he turned and walked back to his chair. She was half-tempted to touch herself again, just to show him that he couldn't control her, but despite her defiance, she couldn't imagine actually following through now that she knew he would be aware of what she was doing. Instead, she huffed defiantly and rolled over, turning her back on him. She expected that mortification and annoyance would keep her awake but her body felt limp and heavy after her climax and she was asleep within minutes.

THE NEXT TIME SHE WOKE, SUNLIGHT POURED THROUGH the uncovered windows. Kalpar was still in his chair, but although his eyes were closed she didn't think he was asleep. When she sat up, his eyes immediately snapped open. Nothing in his expression revealed any emotions about their encounter during the night and for some reason that annoyed her. Her annoyance grew when she climbed out of bed and he immediately rose.

"This really isn't necessary. I just need to attend to my, umm, bodily functions."

He didn't respond and when she stomped into the bathroom, he followed her. Fortunately, the toilet compartment was concealed behind a wall and after inspecting it, he left her alone to attend to her business. Her face was still pink with embarrassment when she emerged and found him waiting in front of the door to the bedroom, his arms crossed.

"Do you wish to bathe again?"

"No, thank you."

"Fine. I am going to take a shower. Do not attempt to leave this room."

"What? No, you can't—"

Her protest fell on deaf ears. He was already unclasping the black belt holding his long knife sheaths and placing it on the bench next to the shower. A second belt followed before he removed his shirt. His shoulders were even wider than she had expected—a lot wider—and she was still staring open-mouthed at the muscular expanse of his bare chest when his hands dropped to his pants. She caught a brief glimpse of a line of dark purple hair before she realized what she was doing and hastily averted her gaze.

She could have sworn she heard a low chuckle before the shower came on. *To hell with this*, she wasn't going to stand around while he took a shower. He spoke just as her hand touched the door.

"If you attempt to leave the room, I will come after you and bring you back into the shower with me. Is that what you want, little human?"

Despite the hint of amusement, his voice was absolutely implacable and she had no doubt he would carry through on his threat. Sighing, she let her hand drop. Instead, she went over to the counter to finish her morning routine. It wasn't until she raised her eyes to the mirror that she realized it was perfectly placed to give her a clear view of the glass-enclosed shower.

He was partially turned away from her, his muscular body glistening as he raised his arms to his head and washed his hair. Then she caught a glimpse of the massive shaft between his legs. His cock hung heavily from his body, almost as thick as her wrist, and she swallowed hard, unable to look away. He wasn't even aroused but she was sure he was bigger than any human male.

Even worse, he chose that moment to turn and she had a clear view of that impressive cock. He had ridges running along both sides of his shaft. Ridges, for heaven's sake! There was something different about the head as well but he shifted his weight before she could quite make it out.

She should look away, she really should, but she couldn't pull her gaze from the massive organ. Even under her father's watchful eye, she'd occasionally met a man who intrigued her a little—but never one who had aroused such a direct sexual interest. Her fingers itched with the desire to wrap around that enormous shaft, to see if she could coax a supposedly impossible erection from it. The thought of him growing even larger beneath her hand was both terrifying and intriguing, and she could feel her body responding to the idea.

He shifted position again as he rinsed away the soap and she gasped. The tip of his penis had changed shape, no longer round but flared at the top. Not that she was an expert on the subject, but she'd never heard of anything like that before. A chill ran down her spine, and she looked up to find him looking directly at her, his eyes blazing silver again.

"I wouldn't have expected an innocent little virgin to be so interested in my anatomy."

His tone was mocking but the heat in his eyes was undeniable. She swallowed hard, then raised her chin.

"I was just curious because it's… different," she said with as much dignity as possible. "There's no harm in looking, especially since you can't… do anything with it."

"Are you really that naive, little human? My cock is not the only way I could give a female pleasure."

Her mouth fell open.

"I-I thought you weren't interested in women."

He started to say something but apparently thought better of it. Instead, he shrugged and leaned forward to turn off the water.

"What are your plans for the day?"

"I'm visiting the children's hospital."

The monthly visits had been a hard-won battle. Her father donated money to various charities as part of his attempt to convince the world that he was a public-spirited businessman. He had reluctantly allowed her to be involved in some of those charities, again because it was good for his image. She had used that motive to corner him into agreeing to the visits by mentioning it to the chair of the hospital benefit during a public event, giving him the impression that her father had already approved.

Her father had been furious, although she doubted anyone else would have noticed that his usual glacial facade had turned even more icy. He had warned the chair that it might be too much for her fragile health, but in the end he'd allowed the visits and they were the highlight of her existence.

Kalpar raised an eyebrow at the announcement but didn't comment, running a towel briskly over all that gleaming purple skin. Heat rushed to her cheeks as she realized she was staring again, avidly watching the towel moving over his body, especially when he ran it casually over that enormous cock, tracing the ridges down to the flared head which had changed shape yet again to a softly pointed tip.

"Constance?"

The amused note was back in his voice. She jumped guiltily and quickly looked away.

"I don't suppose you'd let me go and get dressed?" she asked hopefully.

"You suppose correctly." He pulled on his pants and crossed to the counter, close enough that his masculine scent wrapped around her, and she struggled to maintain a clear head. "But I won't watch you as intently as you've been watching me. Unless you want me to, of course."

CHAPTER 5

Unable to think of a response to Kalpar's provocative comment, Constance fled towards the bedroom. He didn't try to stop her this time, following her there with his shirt and knives in his hands.

"Well?" he asked, raising an eyebrow when she hesitated in front of her wardrobe. "Do you want me to watch?"

For a moment she was actually tempted. The thought of his silver eyes turning white as he watched her remove her nightgown was unexpectedly appealing, but common sense took over.

"Turn around, please."

His lips quirked as he obeyed, moving in front of the bedroom door as he pulled on his shirt at last. Even though his back was turned, her skin still prickled with awareness as she slipped her nightgown over her head. Keeping a wary eye on his back, she picked a pair of panties from a drawer overflowing with lace and color. They were the one indulgence her father permitted when it came to clothing.

She had first arranged to purchase several pairs not long after her eighteenth birthday, hoping to keep it a secret from him. Instead, she'd been summoned to his office the next day.

"Who are these for?" he demanded, holding up a scrap of pink lace.

"No one!" When he only gave her an icy glare, she hurried on. "I know you prefer that I dress modestly, but I wanted something pretty. No one will ever see them," she added hopefully.

To her surprise, he'd agreed to let her keep them. He'd adamantly refused to consider any other changes to her wardrobe since then, but she'd taken some solace in her pretty underthings.

As she pulled on a pair of blue silk panties with a tiny bow at the back, she couldn't help wondering what Kalpar would think of them.

Nothing, she told herself firmly. *He's never going to see them.*

Next she selected another of her long-sleeved high-neck gowns. This one had a slightly wider neck than most of them, enough to reveal a hint of collarbone, and his eyes immediately went to the tiny patch of exposed skin when she told him he could turn around again.

She did her best to ignore him as she moved over to the dressing table and released her hair from the tangled bun. Usually she brushed it before she went to bed and then braided it, but she'd been too disconcerted last night to worry about it. *I'm paying for that now*, she thought, wincing as she started trying to brush out the tangles.

"Do you normally confine your hair?" he asked, startling her.

He had moved silently to her side, staring at the tangled blonde curls cascading down her back.

"Yes. Why?"

"It is quite lovely."

His fingers lightly stroked through her hair until they snagged on a tangle and she winced.

"That's why. I should have braided it last night." She sighed as she checked her wrist com. "It's going to take me forever to get it untangled."

"Allow me."

Before she could stop him, he took the brush out of her hand.

"What are you doing? Give that back!"

"Behave yourself," he said calmly as he set to work.

Almost every nurse she'd ever had had brought her to the brink of tears when brushing her hair. She expected Kalpar would be even more ruthless. Instead, he worked patiently but rapidly, starting at the ends of the long strands and working his way higher with no more than an occasional slight, almost pleasant tug. The process was remarkably soothing, and by the time he was able to run the brush the full length of her curls, she was floating in a pleasurable daze.

"Your hair is quite remarkable."

He put down the brush and repeated the movement with his fingers before wrapping her hair around his hand and giving it another gentle tug, a little harder this time. Her nipples suddenly peaked beneath her gown, responding to the gesture, and she found herself leaning into his hand, instinctively asking for more.

He inhaled sharply, his eyes briefly flashing white, and she froze. What was she thinking?

"I'd better put it up," she said breathlessly.

He gave an abrupt nod and released her. He watched as she pinned it up with the speed of long experience, his face unreadable. When she stood up, he gestured for her to lead the way and then followed her to the sitting room. The table in the small dining alcove to one side of the room had already been set for breakfast—for one person.

She looked at the single place setting, then sighed.

"Why don't you join me for breakfast?"

"You need food more than I do."

"I'm not going to go hungry if that's what you're worried about." She began pulling the lids off the row of dishes waiting on the buffet. "They always send up far too much food, but I stopped fighting it years ago. One of my maids told me they put the extra food to good use."

As he inspected the contents of the dishes, she dug through the cabinet until she found another place setting and added it to the table. She was staring down at it when he came to join her.

"What is it?"

"T-this…" Her voice threatened to break. "This is the first time anyone has ever joined me here."

She'd shared meals with her caregivers while she was in the nursery, but they had been dismissed and she'd been installed in this suite on her twelfth birthday. Since then she'd occasionally entertained a carefully selected female over tea in her sitting room, but that had been the limit of her social interactions.

She took a deep breath, willing back the tears that threatened. Kalpar seemed to recognize her struggle, waiting patiently as she wrested her emotions under control. Then to her surprise he pulled out her chair and seated her before taking the other seat, his manners as refined as any of her father's legitimate associates.

They spoke very little as they ate, but she still took pleasure in his companionship. *Not a companion*, she reminded herself. A paid bodyguard, even if he was the first one to be allowed into her suite rather than standing guard outside it. Even Algar had refused to enter.

After she had finished her breakfast, Kalpar asked her about the upcoming hospital visit.

"I mainly go to visit the children. Some of them are so ill they can never leave the hospital and they're lonely. Even if they have parents, they can't always visit them every day and they don't have many playmates. So I spend time with them and read them stories."

"What kind of stories?"

"All kinds. They seem to be most fascinated by tales of adventure."

"Perhaps because they wish for adventures of their own." He glanced down at his wrist com. "We should be leaving if you are still insistent upon going."

"Of course I'm going," she snapped. "I'll be ready in ten minutes."

He raised a skeptical eyebrow and his doubts proved correct—it took her far more than ten minutes to gather her things. He watched patiently as she assembled her bag of books and the box of brightly decorated cookies the cook had prepared for her.

She would have preferred to make them herself, but although her father had insisted that she learned to cook, he had no intention of letting her mingle with the servants in the kitchens. When she'd asked why he'd bothered to have her taught, he'd coldly informed her that some males required such a skill from their mates.

Will Lord Vexian expect me to cook for him, she wondered bitterly.

Kalpar insisted on carrying both her bag and the cookies as he escorted her to the elevator, then down to the underground parking area. He frowned as he surveyed the area.

"How many people have access to this level?"

"Well, there's my father, of course, along with Warshan and his most trusted team. My bodyguards and my father's bodyguards, plus our drivers. I think that's all." She pointed to the wide doors on the far wall. "My father's senior executives have access to that area, but they aren't allowed back here."

He shook his head.

"I don't like it. Too many unknowns."

His words sent a shiver down her back as they crossed the parking area, the large space suddenly seeming cold and threatening. In addition to her father's carefully displayed vehicles, the garage held various pieces of equipment used to service the vehicles, many of them large enough to conceal an intruder, and she found herself edging closer to him.

He looked down at her and a hint of a smile curved his mouth.

"Don't worry, little human. I won't allow anyone else to trouble you."

Anyone else? She was still wondering what he'd meant by that when her driver hurried over to meet them, but she let it drop, preferring to concentrate on the upcoming visit instead.

CHAPTER 6

alpar sat in the corner of Constance's office, watching her work. Despite the overly elaborate formal furniture, it was actually a working office. Since they'd returned from the hospital, he'd watched her work on a proposal for a charity project, reconcile financial records, and conduct several virtual meetings, also related to various charities. His little human continued to surprise him, proving less and less like his preconceived notion of her with every moment.

Even the hospital had been a revelation. She knew the name of everyone they encountered and made a point of greeting all of them. A few people were less than friendly, but she smiled at them anyway before she moved on. The majority, however, clearly liked her, and as for the children they obviously adored her. Any of them who were capable of moving scrambled over to meet her while the bedridden ones gave her eager smiles.

Even though they weren't there for long, she insisted on spending at least a few minutes with each individual child before gathering them all together for story time.

But it changes nothing, he thought grimly. Although he was also less and less convinced that Marshall had any true concern for his daughter, he clearly considered her a valuable asset and he would be prepared to bargain for her return. Especially if he intended to arrange a mating with Vexian. He found his hand on one of his knives at the thought. Given what he'd heard of the male's proclivities, he doubted it would be a happy union. *Not my business.*

He pushed the unwelcome thought aside as he watched her. She was frowning down at her screen, biting on the end of her stylus. The sight of her pretty lips pursed around it caused another of those unforeseen reactions in his body. Not an actual erection—there was no chance of that—but a rush of warmth as if he were becoming aroused. He mentally cursed as his body reacted, his skin prickling with heat and his nostrils flaring as if he were scenting a potential mate.

Her fresh, clean scent should not have caused such a response, but there was no doubt that... something was happening to his body. Perhaps it was simply due to the previous night when he'd realized she was pleasuring herself beneath the covers. The sensible option would have been to ignore it. Instead, he'd found himself stalking over to the bed and pulling back the sheet. The image of the small hand lodged between her slender thighs was forever imprinted on his brain.

Despite her small size, she was clearly ripe, ready to be mated and bred. He'd been on the verge of insisting that she remove her hand, that she let him explore every inch of her delicious body with his hands and his tongue and his... The realization that there was no hope of anything else had finally brought him to his senses. Yet the heat continued to prickle his skin as he returned to his chair for the rest of a sleepless night.

And then there was his cock. The head of a Catari's cock changed shape for several reasons—to aid in penetration or breeding or simply pleasure—but those changes were only supposed to occur in the presence of his mate. His cock had responded simply to her presence in the room as he showered, and her wide-eyed gaze had sent another surge of awareness over his skin.

Perhaps before he returned to the farm he should make a visit to Drakkar, the Arkanian medic who resided in the mountains to the north of the farm, and make sure there was nothing amiss with his body chemistry.

He was contemplating the prospect when she looked up and found him watching her. The pretty tide of pink flooded her cheeks, and he found himself wondering how far it reached—past her collarbone? As far as those two sweet little breasts?

Her eyes widened as they went to his hand and he belatedly realized he was flipping his knife—a habit he'd picked up many years ago.

"W-what is that for?"

"It's just a habit."

"You need something else to do with your hands." Her color deepened and he suspected she'd suddenly realized the implication in her words. "Don't you have a hobby?"

"Knife throwing."

"Are you serious?"

He flipped his knife again and threw it at the far wall. It landed in the exact center of the ornamental scrollwork, just as he'd intended.

"Wow." Her smile was a little shaky as she watched him retrieve it. "I guess it's a good thing you're on my side."

An unwelcome pang of guilt hit him at her words, and he quickly changed the subject.

"I noticed something unusual at the hospital today. Everyone you came in contact with, from the doctors to the volunteers, was a female."

"That was one of the conditions of the visits. My father decreed that I was not to have contact with any men during my visits. Since he backed up his 'request' with a large donation, they were happy to comply."

"All the members of your charity organizations are female as well."

"All of the ones I have contact with, yes. The only time I have any contact with a man is during the social events he requires me to attend, and even then he monitors every interaction." She peeped at him from under her eyelashes. "That's why I was so curious about the naked male in my shower."

"Indeed. Did my presence also lead to your… behavior last night?"

From the rush of color to her cheeks, he was sure he was right. Ignoring a surge of satisfaction at the knowledge, he rose to his feet.

"It's time for you to eat."

"You know I'm quite capable of determining that for myself. Or are you trying to fatten me up like a calf for the slaughter? To make me a more desirable acquisition for Lord Vexian?"

"You do not need anything to make you more desirable."

The compliment emerged before he could prevent it, drawn by the bitterness in her voice, and she gave him a startled look before she smiled.

"Thank you. As it happens, I am hungry. Shall we dine?"

She came to his side and took his arm. He stared down at the small hand on his arm for a fraction too long before he turned and led her out of the room.

More dishes had been prepared and left in the dining room, but this time the table was actually set for both of them. She gave it a pleased glance before handing him the bottle of wine that had been left chilling.

"Will you open this please?"

"I don't mind, but why don't you have servants attending to you?"

He couldn't imagine Marshall opening his own wine, let alone serving his own food. She sighed.

"It's complicated. My father is very conscious of his station, and by extension mine, but several times over the years I have become... friends with a servant. He dislikes that even more than he dislikes the thought that I might not be living up to my position. Since many of the servants who attend me are also his spies and I dislike the formality he prefers, it has become easier to simply take care of myself." She smiled ruefully as he handed her a plate of delicacies. "Well, perhaps taking care of myself is an exaggeration. I'm simply without visible servants."

"Isn't that lonely?"

"Yes." Her eyes met his across the table, a wealth of sadness in the crystal blue depths. "I have spent much of my life alone but

I have never become accustomed to it."

Her simple statement sent an unexpected pang of sympathy through him, and he was almost glad when she looked down at her plate. He rarely allowed himself to feel sympathy for another. His fellow warriors were the only ones who had earned his loyalty. He stiffened at the thought of them and their interest in his mission. Allowing her to touch his emotions would only make his task more difficult.

He was careful not to meet her gaze as he filled his own plate, keeping his expression stoic and professional as they ate. When she reached for a second helping, he permitted a slight frown.

"You should eat more slowly."

"I can't help it. Everything is so delicious tonight. Perhaps it's the company."

He grunted, refusing to respond to the shy smile in her eyes, and she bit her lip and looked down. *Fuck.*

"I understand. I have eaten too many meals alone."

The acknowledgement was undoubtedly a mistake, but he found it hard to regret them when he was rewarded with a radiant smile. Determined to move to less personal matters, he changed the subject to the calls she had conducted over the afternoon. She was willing to be diverted and they spent the rest of the meal discussing what was clearly a favorite subject for her.

They sat at the table talking long after they'd finished eating. They'd also emptied the bottle of wine and she swayed slightly when she finally yawned and rose to her feet.

"Time for bed."

"Very well." He joined her, tucking her hand in his arm once more—merely to support her, he assured himself. "What is it tomorrow? Widows? Orphans? Some helpless but appealing animal?"

She giggled, leaning slightly against his side, and drawing a corresponding smile from him.

"Nothing so interesting. I have a weekly grooming appointment."

"Grooming?"

"My father insists that I be buffed and polished like one of his vehicles - although unlike them, I am never allowed to be driven." She leaned closer as they reached her bedroom. "I almost wish…"

"Wish what, my little human?"

She came to a halt, looking up at him, her eyes like stars in the dim room.

"I almost wish that…" A great shuddering sigh escaped her and she shook her head. "Never mind. It's foolish to long for things that cannot be."

She started to turn away but he held her easily in place, pulling her closer to his body.

"What do you wish, Constance?"

"That all of my first times were not going to belong to Lord Vexian. I've never even been kissed."

Despite the warning bells chiming in his head, he couldn't resist the shy invitation in her eyes and he lowered his mouth to hers. He'd intended nothing more than a brief touch, but as soon as their lips met, pleasure exploded through his system. When her lips parted beneath his, he couldn't resist sweeping inside to taste her sweetness. She made a small sound of pleasure, her arms sliding up to his neck as she pressed her soft little body against his.

He groaned, and deepened the kiss. Instead of pulling back, she responded eagerly. Heat suffused his skin but he ignored it as he took more of what she so willingly offered. Cradling her head with one hand, he used the other to bring her even closer —close enough that he could feel the small hard peaks of her nipples against his chest.

His cock stirred—a slight but perceptible movement—and the unexpected reaction flared through his veins, shocking him out of the moment. It should have been impossible, but his body was responding to her. What was she doing to him? How could he have been so foolish as to kiss her?

He tore his mouth away, a sudden growl building in his throat, and he clamped down ruthlessly on both his anger and the lust surging through his body. Her eyes flew open as he took a step back.

"Please... don't..."

"This is a dangerous game, little human," he ground out.

"But..."

"Constance, go to bed. Please."

Perhaps she heard the desperation in his voice because she stopped arguing. She studied his face for a moment, her hand pressed to her mouth, then nodded.

"I need to change," she said quietly.

"Go ahead."

He turned his back to her, even though it was the last thing he wanted to do. He wanted more, more of those sweet little lips and that delightful little body and that shy enthusiasm. *I can't.* No matter how much he wanted to explore the connection between them, he still had a mission to perform.

"I've changed. I'm going to brush my teeth."

He knew he should follow her, but he desperately needed breathing space, an opportunity to consider his conflicting emotions. He compromised by going as far as the bathroom door, standing in the open doorway and keeping his back to her.

His body was still throbbing from the unexpected sensations, and he found himself imagining standing behind her and watching her face in the bathroom mirror, his hand cupping one of those sweet little breasts as he explored the curve of her neck with his mouth. *Fuck.* He could smell her arousal in the air, just as he had last night. That too was something that shouldn't have happened. He should not have been so aware of her response—a mate's response.

No. The very thought was impossible.

He heard her approach, but he couldn't bring himself to move until a small hand lightly touched his back.

"I'm ready for bed."

She was using the same pleasant, neutral voice she'd used at the hospital when dealing with unfriendly people. Recognizing that broke something in him, but he forced himself to nod and step aside. He heard the soft rustle of sheets as he returned to the chair he'd used the night before, but when he finally turned around, she was still sitting upright, watching him.

"You didn't do anything wrong," she said quietly. "I wanted you to kiss me and I'm still glad that you did. You didn't betray my trust."

"You think that's why—"

He bit off the words, and she nodded.

"Yes. I know you're an honorable male, Kalpar."

Her words cut into him like one of his knives, rendering him silent. She didn't seem to expect a response, a tiny smile curving her lips before she finally lay down and closed her eyes. He wanted nothing more than to go to her, even if it were just to hold her while she slept. Instead, he settled back in his chair and prepared to keep watch over her instead.

CHAPTER 7

Once again Constance watched in the mirror as Adele made the final adjustments to her dress. The passage of a week had not changed her opinion of the dress—it was as heavy and unflattering as ever—but at least she was no longer quite so pale. There was another change as well, and Adele hummed thoughtfully as she finished lacing the elaborate ribbons across the front of the outer robe.

"You appear to have put on a little weight, Miss Thompson. A needed improvement," the seamstress added hastily, clearly afraid that Constance would take offense.

She was amused rather than offended, smiling at Kalpar as their eyes met in the mirror. He was extremely diligent about making sure she ate. She'd also found that she enjoyed eating much more when she was sharing a meal with him. After a brief hesitation, he returned her smile and she bit back a sigh.

The week had been confusing in many ways and he was the main source of her confusion. They had been together the entire time, just as he had promised, but she sometimes felt as if she didn't know any more about him than she had when her father had presented him to her.

But that isn't entirely true, she thought, a reminiscent smile curving her lips. Now she knew what he looked like naked, she knew how he kissed, and she had experienced his kindness every day. Despite that, she still had the impression he was concealing something from her. He'd revealed almost nothing about his previous life, changing the subject whenever she'd brought it up, and she hadn't pressed him.

She also hadn't had the courage to suggest repeating their kiss and he hadn't offered, but she'd seen him looking at her mouth often enough, his silver eyes flashing white, that she was sure he'd thought about it as often as she had. Perhaps after this wretched ball was over...

She'd never been a fan of the high-profile social events her father favored, always feeling tongue-tied and ill at ease, but knowing that she would be meeting the male her father had chosen for her only made it worse. *Maybe he isn't as bad as I've heard*, she thought, but her eyes went back to the mirror, studying the huge figure of her bodyguard, standing patiently in the corner of her room. The severe formal uniform her father had ordered suited him, accentuating the strong lines of his body and that handsome alien face.

Her father would never countenance such a match, but she couldn't help a wistful thought for what might have been. Despite her lack of knowledge about his past, she wouldn't have hesitated to accept a match with him. Not that he necessarily returned her interest, of course. But then their eyes met in the mirror again and his flashed white. Yes, he was interested.

Adele performed one final check, making sure that the high back collar of the robe hadn't damaged her elaborate upswept hairdo, then stepped back.

"All you need now are the jewels and you're ready."

"They're in the box on the table—"

Kalpar brought them over before she finished speaking and Adele opened the box, giving an awed gasp.

"Very nice indeed, and a perfect complement to the dress."

The seamstress carefully fastened the heavy necklace around her neck. Elaborate gold scrollwork framed glittering purple jewels she didn't recognize. The overall effect was almost barbaric in its splendor and Adele was right, it did complement the dress—although, like the dress, it was too heavy and ornate to suit her. A matching tiara was pinned into her intricate hairstyle and her head immediately started to ache, but she forced a smile.

"Thank you, Adele."

"Not at all, Miss Thompson. I trust you will enjoy the ball."

The seamstress bobbed her head and left, leaving her alone with Kalpar.

"What do you think?" she asked him.

He was standing behind her and she watched in the mirror as he lightly touched her hair, then stroked his hand down the fragile column of her neck—the only skin exposed by the dress. His hand lingered on her neck, his thumb gently stroking the curve from ear to shoulder. It was the first time he'd touched her since the kiss, and she had to fight not to lean into his hand.

His touch sent pleasurable shivers racing down her spine, but at least the heavy gown concealed the fact that her nipples had stiffened. His nostrils flared and he took an abrupt step back.

"I think your father will be pleased."

"But not you?"

Her attempt at a teasing note fell flat and he shook his head.

"You know I prefer your hair down."

Their eyes met again. The exception to the moratorium he seemed to have placed on touching her was her hair. He had brushed it for her every morning, working out the tangles before running his fingers through it to "check" for any remaining knots—a process that always lasted a considerable time. Not that she had the least objection, of course.

"Considering how much time and how many products were required to get it to this state, I suspect you will have your work cut out for you tomorrow."

"I—Yes. Shall we go?"

She nodded, wishing she could take his arm as he went to open the door, but the fitting had taken place in one of the rooms on the main floor of the penthouse and there were sure to be a number of servants around. Instead, she raised her head as much as she could under the weight of the tiara, straightened her shoulders and went to join her father.

An hour later her stomach churned as she descended the grand staircase into a glittering ballroom. Tiny white lights were sprinkled over almost every inch of the ballroom, reflecting in the hundreds of holographic bubbles that floated through the air. Port Cantor's elite filled the opulent space, sipping champagne and exchanging meaningless smiles.

Her father had chosen to arrive separately and she was alone except for Kalpar's reassuring presence. He was the correct two steps back and to the side, but the knowledge that he was there gave her courage. His imposing frame radiated strength and she clung to that amidst the dizzying splendor.

As they reached the foot of the stairs, Ellen, one of the women from the hospital charity, came to speak to her, a friendly smile on her lips, and she relaxed a little. She encountered several other volunteers as she moved through the crowd, although not all of them were as friendly as Ellen. No matter how hard she worked, her father's reputation overshadowed everything she did.

Her father was waiting for her next to a set of doors on one side of the ballroom, an icy smile on his lips.

"Constance. I'm so glad you could join us. Finally." Even though he had been the one to insist that they make separate entrances, his disapproval was clear and she flinched. "Now that you are here, I would like you to meet Lord Vexian."

Dread coiled low in her belly as a hulking alien stepped forward. Even though Lord Vexian was not the only non-human present, his appearance was jarring—mandibles protruded on either side of a prominent jaw and lidless black eyes seemed to bore straight through her. A long black tongue flicked out to trace his mandibles, the leer unmistakable even on that terrifying face.

"She appears very soft." His voice had a grating note, like a metal part that needed oiling.

Soft? Was that intended as a compliment? She chose to assume it was and forced herself to incline her head graciously. "You're too kind, my lord."

"Not at all."

The ridged edges of one of Vexian's powerful claws closed around her wrist. He wasn't hurting her, but the threat was there. He tugged her forward, inspecting her like a piece of livestock, and she wondered hysterically if he was going to want to examine her teeth as well. Bile rose in her throat as he leaned closer, his cold, musty breath ghosting over her cheek.

Kalpar made a slight abortive movement but thankfully he remained in position. She couldn't bear the thought that he might suffer the same fate as Algar.

Vexian's claw traced the high neck of her under gown.

"Her face is satisfactory. But what does this conceal, I wonder?" He looked over at her father and clicked his mandibles. "You cannot expect me to make an acquisition without a thorough inspection."

Inspection? Surely her father would never permit such a thing. To her despair, he only nodded coolly.

"Of course. Come this way."

Her father opened the door behind him, and her horror intensified as she realized why he had chosen this position. Her stomach roiled as she followed him down the corridor, Lord Vexian's clawed hand an unwelcome weight on the small of her back. Though she kept her chin high, every step felt like a lead weight dragging her down into an inescapable nightmare.

Halfway down the hall, her father opened another door into an empty study with a carved wooden desk and several large leather chairs arranged in front of a blackened fireplace. Vexian leered down at her, his lipless mouth stretched in a grotesque facsimile of a smile. "After you, my dear."

She hesitated on the threshold but her father's icy expression brooked no argument. She forced herself to enter, the dark wood paneling and lingering traces of smokestick fumes giving the room a suffocating air. Her father paid no attention to her hesitation, looking past her to Kalpar.

"You are dismissed until I summon you again."

She couldn't prevent herself from giving him a quick terrified look. He hesitated for a moment, his eyes flashing white as they met hers. But then he inclined his head, his face an inscrutable mask as he stepped back into the corridor and closed the door behind him.

"Now then," Vexian grated, making himself at home in one of the large chairs as he gave her an expectant leer. "Please remove your gown so I may examine my potential bride's assets more... intimately."

Her stomach churned as her father settled into the chair across from Vexian without any objection. How could this possibly be the same man who had always been so adamant that she cover her body? She gave him an imploring look, but he met it coldly.

"I have preserved you for precisely this moment. This is your opportunity to prove your worth."

Numb with despair, she fumbled at the elaborate lacing of the over robe but her fingers were shaking too hard to untie it. Her father's face grew increasingly icy, but Vexian chuckled as he rose and joined her.

"Allow me."

One swipe of a terrifyingly sharp claw and the ribbons simply fell apart. He raised his thankfully closed claws to her shoulders and pushed the robe off of them, the weight of the fabric carrying it quickly to the ground. She felt horribly exposed, even though the heavy silk under gown still covered her, but there was worse to come.

Vexian circled her, once again studying her as if she were a piece of prime livestock, then looked over at her father.

"This garment may still conceal unacceptable flaws."

Her father would never permit Vexian to go that far, would he? But once again he ignored her unspoken plea and nodded.

"You may remove it."

A terrified whimper escaped her lips and her father frowned, but Vexian only laughed again before slicing a claw across the second set of ribbons. Fabric whispered over her skin as the heavy satin slipped down over her shoulders to pool at her feet. Adele had provided a strapless one piece undergarment that matched the gown so she wasn't completely naked but she'd never felt so exposed in her entire life.

Her father surveyed her with an air of clinical detachment as Vexian made another circle. This time he paused in front of her. He played with the ornate necklace for a moment before running a claw across the upper edge of the undergarment. She couldn't prevent herself from shuddering, and his tongue flicked out again.

"She is quite small," Vexian said. "I'm not convinced she can take the full size of a Ctharan. It could be... challenging."

Despite his objection, his eyes were fixed on her breasts, the lust on his face obvious. Her father shrugged.

"A human female's body is designed to stretch. I'm sure she can be trained to take you. And wouldn't that be preferable to a female who has already been used by others?"

His clinical response only added to the nightmarish quality of the scene.

"She is quite untouched?"

"Completely. You will be the first to possess her in every way."

Vexian pushed a claw thoughtfully against the slight swell of her breast and another whimper escaped. He laughed and looked over at her father.

"It appears that you have already trained her to be compliant at least. Such a refreshing change from a Ctharan female."

I'm not compliant, she screamed in her head, but the words refused to emerge from her mouth.

"Compliance is her most valuable trait." Her father's words were clearly intended as a warning and she shuddered again. "Are you satisfied with your inspection?"

Vexian chittered thoughtfully as he traced the edge of the undergarment again and she prayed desperately that he wouldn't demand that she remove that as well. But he shook his head and turned away.

"For now. However, I will require a medical exam and I expect to be present for that exam."

A whole new level of horror washed over her, but once again her father only nodded before giving her a dismissive look.

"Agreed. You may get dressed and go, Constance. I'll summon you when Lord Vexian and I have concluded our negotiations."

She scooped up the discarded gold silk gown and flung it over her head, then fled the suffocating study. Tears blurred her vision but she ran anyway, her only thought to get away. She careened around a corner and ran directly into Kalpar's solid frame.

His hands gripped her shoulders to steady her, the warmth of his hands penetrating her cold skin.

"Constance? What—"

She crumpled against him, finally allowing the shame and despair she'd bottled up to erupt in a torrent of tears.

CHAPTER 8

Kalpar paced the dimly lit corridor, fighting his instinctive urge to protect Constance. He'd almost betrayed his feelings twice now—the first time when Vexian had dared to lay his hands on her and pulled her closer and the second time in the study when she'd given him that despairing look.

He'd barely managed to control himself long enough to remember that if Marshall fired him—or tried to eliminate him—no one would be left to protect her. The fact that it would also compromise his mission was a distinct afterthought. *Fuck.* Despite every attempt he'd made over the past week to distance himself, he was far too concerned with this fragile human.

The fact that he'd also spent the week fighting the urge to explore the physical attraction between them had only made it worse. He desperately wanted to kiss her again, to explore that soft little body, to find out if his body would truly respond to her. He'd managed to resist the urge, although he'd had to make one change in his guardianship—he no longer insisted that he accompany her into the bathing room or that she remain while he showered. He'd simply left the door open between the two rooms instead and soothed his conscience with the knowledge that he could be at her side in seconds.

Even without her physical presence in the room, there had been two separate occasions when he was showering and just the thought of her had sent a tremor through his cock. He was still not convinced that she could be his mate, although he was beginning to suspect that his body was trying to tell him something. But the lesson he'd learned from that brief period of youthful lust was that a mere physical reaction was not enough to satisfy him.

He refused to consider the fact that her kind heart and gentle spirit already called to him as much as her sweet body. And beneath that delicate exterior, he sensed a strength, a resilience that belied her sheltered upbringing. He shook his head, banishing the treacherous thoughts. There was no room for such fancies, not in his world. He was a warrior, and she was a means to an end. That was all there was to it.

Wasn't it?

He took another turn down the corridor, pausing outside the study door again. He couldn't hear anything, but hopefully that was a good sign. If she cried out, he knew he wouldn't be able to prevent himself from going to her.

On his next circuit he noticed a door embedded in the wall paneling and, in an attempt to distract himself, tried to open it. It opened easily enough to reveal another hallway, this one distinctly different from the opulent corridor he had been pacing. The floor and walls were bare concrete and the lights embedded in the walls bare and utilitarian. The space was clearly designed to provide access for servants, and after another check to make sure that all was quiet in the study, he decided to make a quick survey and find out where it went.

He returned just as a crying Constance raced down the corridor. He grabbed her before she could crash into him and she collapsed against him, crying as though her heart was breaking. The embroidered robe had disappeared and the gold under gown was falling down across one fragile shoulder. Rage surged through him, magnified by his guilt at having left her alone with those two bastards. They would pay for her distress, but getting her out of here was more urgent.

He swept her into his arms, cradling her trembling form against his chest as he returned to the servant's hallway. She clung to him, her face buried in the crook of his neck. He could feel the dampness of her tears against his skin and increased his pace, determined to get her away from this wretched place as swiftly as possible.

They didn't encounter anyone before emerging into the cool night air. The area was clearly intended for deliveries, but a fleet of vehicles were parked on the other side of a neatly trimmed hedge and he recognized the hover vehicle in which they'd arrived. Because of his position in the household, the doors opened to his touch. When he tried to put her down on the seat she clung to his neck, unwilling to let go of him.

"Let me go, sweetheart, so we can get out of here."

She gave another muffled sob, but she released him and he slid behind the controls. The engine hummed to life, and he gunned the accelerator, quickly taking them higher than was strictly legal. The city lights blurred past in a kaleidoscope of colors as she buried herself against his side again.

"Can you tell me what happened?" he asked gently.

His grip tightened on the controls as she sobbed out the story of what had happened in the study. With each word, his anger grew, a simmering rage that threatened to boil over.

"He doesn't care about me at all," she choked out between sobs. "I-I always hoped that he was so controlling because he was trying to protect me. All he wanted was to make sure I'd fetch the highest price. But I can't marry Lord Vexian, I can't. Please, Kalpar, you have to help me."

"I won't let that happen," he growled, his voice low and dangerous. "I'll keep you safe, Constance. I promise."

As they drove on into the night, her sobs gradually subsided as exhaustion overtook her. She slumped against the seat, her breathing finally evening out as she drifted into a fitful sleep. He couldn't bear to see her like this, broken and defeated by the cruelty of her own father.

What was he going to do? He had to get her away from her father's clutches, but he also needed the information Marshall possessed. But perhaps he could turn this to his favor. It would require moving up his timeline, but he could hide her away somewhere safe and then use her disappearance to his advantage.

He was sure that her father would be desperate to get her back, if only to complete his deal with Lord Vexian. The Ctharan obviously possessed something that Marshall wanted. Even though he had no intention of returning her, perhaps he could use that desperation, manipulate the situation to extract the information he needed. It was a risky move, but it was the only option he could come up with that would allow him to protect both her and the warriors back on the farm.

He descended to a legal height and took a circuitous route away from the wealthy districts at the center of Port Cantor. As soon as he found a deserted lot, he switched out the luxury hovercar for a nondescript, common vehicle, putting his old skills to use. He followed a meandering path through the less savory areas of the city, then switched vehicles again. Constance slept through most of the journey, although she whimpered in her sleep and her body twitched restlessly.

She woke up during the last transfer, giving him a dazed look.

"Where are we going?"

"Somewhere safe," he replied, his tone low and reassuring. "Away from your father and Lord Vexian."

She nodded, and when she fell asleep again she seemed more peaceful.

He doubled back several times to make sure they weren't being followed before finally arriving at an old warehouse down by the fishing docks. Pulling around to the small side alley, he entered a code into the keypad and drove inside as it slid open.

The warehouse was dark and musty, smelling of brine and creaking with the sigh of the tide, but it was quiet and deserted. Constance was still asleep so he carried her through the maze of crates and equipment to a set of rickety stairs leading to the second floor.

At the top was a small apartment, sparsely furnished but equipped with the basic necessities. He had set it up weeks ago as a secure safe house, a hidden refuge where he could retreat if needed. Now it would shelter both of them. Laying her gently on the bed, he did a quick check to make sure that everything was as he'd left it. He should begin planning his next steps, figuring out how to contact Marshall and set his plan in motion. Instead, he found himself lingering by the bed, looking down at her face in the dim light.

She looked so vulnerable in sleep, her fine features still marked by the tears she had shed earlier. An unfamiliar ache filled his chest. Before he could stop himself, he reached out and tenderly brushed a strand of tangled hair back from her cheek. His instincts urged him to protect her, to keep her close, and he sank down on the edge of the mattress, weariness creeping over him as he watched the steady rise and fall of her breathing.

He knew he should move, should begin preparations, but he couldn't make himself leave her. She was so fragile, this little human who had so unexpectedly entangled herself in his thoughts. When she whimpered in her sleep, her body twitching, he swore under his breath then moved further on to the mattress before picking her up and cradling her in his arms.

She settled down again and he decided he would permit himself this brief moment. Just for tonight, there were no missions, no conflicting goals, just the two of them here in this hidden refuge. He knew it couldn't last, but for now he let the world fall away and yielded to the simple pleasure of holding her close as he surrendered to sleep.

CHAPTER 9

Constance woke slowly, blinking in the dim light filtering through a dingy window. For a moment she was disoriented, confused by the lumpy mattress and rough blanket. Then memory came flooding back—her father's cruelty, her vile intended fiancé, and Kalpar whisking her away into the night.

She started to bolt upright but then Kalpar was there. He'd been the lumpy mattress beneath her. She gave a sob of relief and his arms closed tightly around her as she began to shake.

"Shh, shh, you're safe, sweetheart. We're in my safe house. You're safe here."

She took several deep breaths as she absorbed that, and he loosened his hold so that he could run his hand up and down her back in long, soothing strokes.

"Y-you kept me safe. You got me away from my father and Lord Vexian," she said, tilting her face up to his. "How can I ever thank you?"

"No need," he murmured, his breath warm on her skin and his eyes glowing white.

Yielding to impulse, she lifted high enough to press her lips against his. He froze for a moment, then groaned and responded, his tongue sweeping into her mouth and sending excitement racing through her. Her nipples tingled and she pressed her breasts against that hard chest, seeking relief from the increasing ache.

Then he was pulling back, gently detaching her arms from around him.

"You should eat something," he said gruffly, not meeting her eyes. "There's food and water."

Heat suffused her cheeks as she looked away. How could she have been so forward? She focused on her surroundings in an attempt to relieve her embarrassment. They were in a sparse room, shabby but clean, that contained nothing but the bed. Through an open doorway she could see another minimally furnished room containing a crooked table and two chairs.

She caught the tang of salt and heard the gentle lap of water and decided they must be close to the fishing port. But why here? And why did he have a safe house?

"You said this was a safe house?"

Her voice came out a little husky but firm enough.

"Yes. I was trained to always have an escape plan."

"Trained?"

"By the military. I served in the Alliance forces."

The fact that he was a warrior didn't surprise her, but she wondered why he'd never mentioned it.

"I served on Vizal," he added, his voice reluctant. "It's not a time I care to remember."

Ah. She'd been too young—and too sheltered—to know many details, but even she knew that it had been a long, painful war with many losses. He rose to his feet, his face stern, clearly through with the discussion.

"I will prepare food. There is a sanitary facility through there if you need it."

He disappeared into the other room without looking at her, and she sighed and started to stand. Her dress immediately threatened to slide down and she had to grab it. Hopefully Kalpar had something to replace the cut ribbons.

The bathroom too was worn but clean. She washed her face and hands and rinsed out her mouth before catching a glimpse of herself in the small tarnished mirror. Yikes. The tiara was still embedded in the tangled curls falling down around her pale face and she suddenly recognized the cause of the dull ache in her temples. When she tried to pull it free, it felt as if all her hair were going to come with it.

Clutching the tiara with one hand and her gown with the other, she hobbled into the other room. In addition to the table and chairs, there were a few ancient appliances along one wall and a lumpy couch. Sunlight flooded in from a row of high windows, open to let in the fresh sea breeze.

"I need help," she announced and Kalpar turned to look at her.

The severe mask he'd assumed disappeared as his lips quirked.

"Indeed."

"I don't suppose you have a brush? Or some scissors?"

"We are not going to cut your hair," he said immediately, frowning at her. "I can free the tiara."

"If you say so." She took a half-step towards him and almost tripped when the dress slipped again. "I need something to hold up this dress as well."

"One problem at a time. Sit down."

She took a seat at the small table and he began working on her hair. It reminded her of the mornings when he'd brushed out her hair, but this was different. Although they'd been alone in her rooms, she'd always been conscious of the fact that they were in her father's house and she suspected Kalpar had been as well. Now they were completely alone, and for the first time in her life she had absolutely no supervision.

Under any other circumstances she would have been terrified, but although a tiny shiver skated across her skin, it was not from fear. Perhaps he felt it too. He worked as carefully as always, but he took his time and she was sure he was letting his fingers linger in her hair and drift across her neck and cheek. Each brush of his skin against hers added to her excitement, and by the time he placed the tiara on the table, her nipples were stiff and tingling and excitement pulsed low in her stomach.

"There," he said, his voice rough.

He stroked her hair, letting his fingers massage her scalp, and she gave in to another foolish impulse and turned her head to press a quick kiss against his hand.

"Thank you."

He didn't immediately whip his hand away as she suspected he might. Instead, he cupped her cheek and raised her face until she was looking up at him.

"I told you that you didn't need to thank me."

"I know, but I do thank you. For everything."

She nestled her cheek against his hand and he let it linger for another moment before abruptly clearing his throat and turning away. She decided to count it as progress anyway and smiled as she watched him move efficiently around the small kitchen area.

The food was simple but unexpectedly delicious, although he shrugged away her compliment. After they finished eating he sat back, regarding her thoughtfully.

"We should discuss our next steps."

We? Her heart skipped a beat at the prospect but she nodded as calmly as possible.

"What do you think we should do? Where should we go?"

He pulled out one of his knives, flipping it thoughtfully.

"I have... contacts outside the city. We could travel to the countryside and lie low for a while. It won't be luxurious but you'll be safe."

"That's all I want," she said sincerely. As long as she was free of her father's control, nothing else mattered.

"It's for the best if we leave soon. I'll make the arrangements."

She nodded, eager to be away from Port Cantor. They seemed to be well hidden, but she didn't want to make the mistake of underestimating her father's resources. She had no doubt he was doing everything in his power to find her. *But not because he wants me back*, she thought bitterly. *So he can sell me to Vexian.*

She just wished she knew why. He'd dangled her in front of other men before but it had been a game—this time there was an intensity in his actions she didn't understand. No, the sooner they were away from here, the better.

The thought of plunging into the unknown made her a little nervous, but knowing that Kalpar would be with her was immensely comforting. She tried to decide if there was some way she could help and remembered the jewelry.

"So you think you could sell the necklace and tiara?"

"I don't think it would be wise—they are too recognizable. I might be able to arrange something with the individual gems but even then it would be a risk. Don't worry, sweetheart, I have enough funds to cover the trip."

A surge of warmth filled her at the endearment, but she only nodded, doing her best not to blush.

They passed the day quietly. Kalpar left briefly to gather supplies and she paced anxiously the entire time he was gone. When he returned, she convinced him to let her cook. Neither the supplies nor the equipment resembled the ones in her lessons, but the results were passable enough. She was surprised at how much pleasure it gave her to watch him eat the food she'd prepared, and she was suddenly glad her father had insisted, even if his motives had been entirely different.

Kalpar ate readily, but she sensed a distance in him that hadn't been there before. She wished she knew what caused it. Was he having second thoughts about helping her? Was it possible he regretted leaving her father's employ? He paid extremely well, and his employees enjoyed a certain degree of prestige. No, she was sure that wasn't it, but she didn't have the courage to ask what was troubling him.

"I don't think it would be a good idea to turn on any lights up here," he said as the sun began to set, washing the room in golden light. "There's no way to cover the windows and I don't want to attract attention."

"Me either," she said quickly.

"Why don't you have an early night?" he said gruffly. "I hope we can leave at first light."

"What about you?"

"I have some work to do in the warehouse. There are no windows down there so it should be safe enough."

"Is there anything I can do to help?"

His face softened for a moment.

"No, sweetheart. Just get some rest."

After he disappeared downstairs, she lay in the darkness listening to him move around. Sleep was a long time coming, her mind filled with questions about their destination—and about him. Everything he'd said made it sound as if he intended to stay with her, but he hadn't explicitly said that he would. She desperately wanted him to stay, wanted to explore the connection between them and see where it went. With that wistful thought she finally drifted off.

She woke an unknown time later, her heart pounding. She'd been dreaming that her father and Vexian had been chasing her and every time she turned a corner they were waiting for her.

Since the sky outside the window was dark and she could still hear Kalpar moving around downstairs, she couldn't have been asleep long.

Still shaking from the dream, she decided to seek out Kalpar's comforting presence instead of trying to go back to sleep, fumbling for her dress in the dark. He had "fixed" her dress by slicing off the bottom six inches as well as both sleeves, and turned one of the sleeves into a sash. At her request he'd also cut a small wedge out of the neckline, and even after the incident with Vexian, it felt shockingly risqué to have her entire collarbone exposed.

She dressed quickly, eager to see him. When she opened the door at the top of the stairs, her sash began to slip. As she paused to retie it, his voice drifted up to her. Was someone else here? Her heart skipped a beat, but then she realized he must be on his communicator. She gave a relieved sigh, but then his words reached her.

"...yes, I have her here. She's unharmed." A pause. "No, I haven't told her anything."

She froze. He was talking about her. A cold feeling settled in the pit of her stomach.

"I'll bring her to you in the morning. Have the payment ready."

His voice was clipped and businesslike, strange to her.

The cold feeling turned to ice. Who was he taking her to? Payment for what?

Her lips felt numb as betrayal swamped her. She'd been foolish enough to trust him and now he was making some kind of deal involving her. Was he selling her to her father? To Vexian?

Fighting back tears, she started to hurry down the steps. She had to get away before he "delivered" her. She had no idea where she was going to go or who she could turn to—she only knew she had to run.

In her haste she misjudged the bottom step. Her foot caught and a startled cry escaped her lips as she went sprawling, cracking her head against the concrete floor. The room spun around her as she lay there, too dazed to move. And then it was too late—Kalpar was bending over her.

CHAPTER 10

*A*s soon as Kalpar heard the soft cry, he knew Constance had overheard his conversation.

"Tomorrow," he said curtly and ended the call as he hurried over to the stairs.

Panic filled him when he saw her sprawled at the bottom, blood covering her face, only abating a little when he kneeled next to her and she gave him a betrayed look before her eyes closed. *Fuck.* Although he doubted she'd heard the entire conversation, he suspected she'd heard enough to be aware that he hadn't told her the entire truth.

An unusual feeling of guilt washed over him as he gently gathered her limp body into his arms. Her eyes fluttered open again, and she regarded him with a mix of fear and resignation.

"Why?" she whispered hoarsely.

The need to protect his fellow warriors conflicted with his protective feelings for this small human female, and he took refuge in dealing with the immediate situation.

"You're injured. Let me tend to you first."

She whimpered as he carried her up the stairs to the small apartment and more guilt filled him as he remembered that she'd made the same sound after her experience with Vexian and her father. As gently as he could, he laid her on the threadbare sofa. Despite his excellent night vision, he decided to take the risk of turning on a small lamp, masking it with a worn towel.

Ignoring her soft protest, he ran his hands quickly over her body, checking for injuries. She had a gash on her forehead and a badly skinned knee but otherwise she was intact. Thank the gods.

He fetched another towel and a bowl of water and began washing the blood from her head and leg. He was as gentle as possible, but she still flinched several times as he cleaned the wounds. She didn't cry out, only watched him with those huge blue eyes, dark with pain and betrayal.

After he fastened a bandage around her head, she lay back, her eyes closed, exhaustion and pain etched on her pale face. His chest ached at the sight. The last thing he wanted was to cause her more pain and suffering.

"Rest now," he said gruffly, covering her with a thin blanket. "We'll talk when you've recovered some strength."

Her eyes opened, crystal tears shimmering in their depths.

"There's nothing left to talk about," she whispered. "It was foolish to think that I could escape. To think that I could trust someone."

"I wasn't going to betray you."

But he had been planning to use her. Perhaps she heard the guilt in his voice because she simply closed her eyes and turned her face away without responding.

Unable to stand the silence, he rose to his feet and started pacing, his mind churning. The image of her body at the bottom of the stairs kept flashing before his eyes, along with the terror he'd felt at the sight. He'd promised to protect her, not cause her harm.

With a sigh, he sank down on one of the rickety kitchen chairs and watched the steady rise and fall of her chest as he tried to sort through the tangled mess of duty and emotion filling him. He didn't think she slept, and eventually her eyes fluttered open, regarding him solemnly.

"I owe you an explanation."

She said nothing, just continued to watch him with those dark blue eyes that saw far too much.

"I didn't set out to deceive you, but my intentions were never pure. Originally I only thought of you as a means to protect my fellow warriors, or at least I tried to think of you that way. I was never very successful."

"Fellow warriors?" she whispered, her eyes shadowed.

"I told you I served during the war on Vizal. Ten years of hell. My first squad commander was a charming male who was secretly engaged in trafficking females." The familiar guilt that he'd been blind to the male's activities washed over him, but he pushed it aside. "After he was arrested I was assigned to another squad. Commander Temel is the finest officer—the finest male—I have ever known. He has always put our needs before his own, even after the war ended."

Unable to keep still, he rose and paced across the room again.

"All of us had... trouble adjusting to civilian life and he was determined to find a way to help us. He eventually purchased a farm, or rather several farms, many of them abandoned, in the hope that working on the land away from the city would help heal us."

"Did it?" she asked softly.

She'd pushed herself upright while he paced, her face pale but determined as she watched him.

"I'm not sure that I will ever be healed," he said honestly, "but most of our squad has managed to find peace."

And mates, but he wasn't ready to bring up that subject.

"I'm glad it helped, but what does that have to do my father? Or me?"

"On at least two occasions, your father has sent someone to infiltrate the farm."

"I don't understand. Why?"

"We don't know—which is why I am here. To find out what he's searching for, and what he intends to do if he finds it."

"And you thought I was the key?" A bitter smile twisted her pretty lips. "I never thought he cared a great deal for me. Now I know he is only interested in using me."

He wished he could disagree, but she was right. What kind of evil bastard only thought of his child as a bargaining tool? That struck a little too close to home and he winced.

"That still means you have value for him," he pointed out reluctantly. "Especially now."

She sighed and tentatively rubbed her head.

"I was thinking that earlier—that Vexian must have something he wants. But I have no more idea of what that might be than you do," she added.

He hesitated, struggling to find the right words.

"You need to understand something. I admit that my original plan was to use you to manipulate him, but when I carried you away from the ball last night, I was only thinking of protecting you from him. It occurred to me afterwards that I could still use you as a bargaining chip, even though I have no intention of turning you over to him. What you heard earlier was a conversation I was having with one of my contacts. I was arranging for them to watch over you while I dealt with your father. Then I was planning on taking you to the farm."

He didn't miss the quick flash of pleasure in her eyes before she frowned.

"Deal with my father? How?"

He sighed and pulled out one of his knives, watching her face as he flipped it.

"I aim to convince him to leave the farm alone. By any means necessary."

"And then you'll just walk away after that? Leave me here?"

Her voice wavered slightly. He hesitated again, then sheathed his knife and went to sit next to her on the couch.

"No. I meant what I said about taking you to the farm—if you still wish to go. I want you to have the chance to live your life on your own terms."

Those blue eyes searched his face. He suddenly felt uncomfortably exposed, but he let her take her time examining him. He'd been as honest as he could. Eventually she sighed and leaned against his shoulder.

"I must admit the idea appeals to me, but I can't imagine that Father will stop looking for me. Not unless he gets what he wants from Vexian. And even then he'd probably want to use me to get some other advantage." She looked up at him, her expression heartbreakingly sad. "It was foolish to think I could ever escape him."

"He can't pursue you to the farm if he doesn't know you're there."

"Don't you think he'll put my disappearance together with your demands?"

She had a point, but he was convinced there was a way out of this situation, for all of them.

"Can you at least agree to go there while you consider your options?"

She closed her eyes, but when they opened, he could see determination in their blue depths.

"You were protecting me, even if your reason for doing so was not what you led me to believe. I will go with you to your farm. If things are not as you say, I will leave."

Relief filled him. He knew he didn't deserve her trust, but she had given it to him nonetheless. His relief was short-lived. The perimeter alarm he'd set up around the safe house beeped once, then again and again. He swore under his breath as he checked his wrist com.

"What is it?"

"We're about to have company," he said grimly as he went to retrieve his getaway bag, quickly throwing in her jewelry and some additional food.

"M-my father?"

"I don't know who else it would be. Someone must have spotted me when I went out this afternoon. Can you walk?"

"Yes," she said at once.

Despite her brave words, she swayed alarmingly as she stood.

"I'll help you as soon as I can, but I need you to support yourself for a few minutes."

"I told you. I can walk."

"Brave little human. Hold on to the couch for a few minutes."

A quick glance showed him that intruders were moving closer, but they were moving slowly, no doubt checking for traps. *They'll find one soon enough*, he thought grimly as he removed the panel concealing the ladder to the roof.

"I need you to climb this ladder. I'll be right behind you and I won't let you fall."

"I believe you," she said quietly as she came to join him.

She took a deep breath, then started to climb. He threw his bag over his shoulder and followed her. Her hands and legs shook, but she kept climbing. As soon as they reached the roof, he closed the trap door and checked the monitors again. It was going to be close.

She didn't protest when he picked her up, then set off across the roof as quickly and silently as he could manage. There was a considerable gap between his warehouse and the one next to it, but he knew he could cover it.

"Don't make a sound," he warned, and then he jumped.

She clutched his neck desperately, but she remained silent. Carrying her threw off his balance and he teetered for a second on the edge of the second roof before he found his balance. He crossed that roof and leaped the smaller distance to the third roof before he checked his com again.

"Time's up," he whispered, crouching down and covering as much of her body as he could.

"Time—"

Her words were interrupted by a loud roar as flames shot up into the night above his warehouse. A few pieces of debris floated through the air, but he had calculated the explosion correctly so that it would only affect his own building.

As soon as the initial explosion was over, he returned to his feet. She gave him a wide-eyed look as he picked her up again.

"You blew up the building?"

"It's no longer a safe house if people know where it's located."

"Oh." She bit her lip as he started across the roof, keeping a cautious eye on the rush of activity below. "You don't think that my f-father was there, do you?"

"No, sweetheart. He sends people to do his dirty work. He doesn't do it himself."

"You're right."

She didn't ask any additional questions but her body relaxed a little against his. He gave her a quick reassuring hug, then concentrated on their escape route.

CHAPTER 11

Constance's head hurt, the throbbing in her temples beginning as soon as she regained consciousness.

Where am I?

The last thing she remembered was the hazy image of a fire, and Kalpar carrying her. She must have passed out at some point because she didn't remember how they'd arrived here... In a flyer, she realized. A very compact flyer which had left her sprawled across Kalpar's lap. Color flooded her cheeks as she tried to sit up, and he gave her a quick smile.

"There's water in the bag, along with a box of pink pills. They're painkillers. Taking one of them should help your head."

She started to nod, then winced. Moving very slowly, she opened the bag at her feet and pulled out the water and the pills. She tipped one onto a palm then gave it a doubtful look.

"After everything that's happened, you're worried about a pill?"

Despite his sardonic tone, she thought she caught a hint of... hurt?

"No, I'm not worried," she said quietly, and swallowed the pill.

It started to work almost immediately, and she sighed with relief as the pain eased. As it ebbed she peered through the window, then gasped. It was still dark outside, but a line of brightness along the horizon forecast the upcoming day. There was enough light for her to make out the imposing range of mountains in front of them. Port Cantor was nowhere in sight.

"W-where are we going?"

"To the farm, just like I said."

"Oh." She thought about that for a moment, then gave him a questioning look. "What about the information you were seeking?"

"An additional day won't make much difference. I wanted to see you safe first," he said gruffly.

He'd put her needs ahead of his own? A lump appeared in her throat, and she leaned over and gave him an impulsive kiss on the cheek.

"Thank you."

He shot her a startled glance, then nodded.

"You're welcome."

"How long will it take to get there?"

"Only another thirty minutes or—" The engine spluttered and he swore viciously. "Or maybe longer. I'm going to fly lower and see if the engine corrects itself."

It didn't, and a few minutes later he was guiding them into a landing as the engine failed completely. He managed to bring them down in a small open clearing and she watched, petrified, as the huge trees surrounding the clearing grew closer and closer. They came to a halt right at the base of one of the largest trees and she sighed with relief, her hand still shaking.

"That was close."

"Too close," he agreed as he opened the door and cool forest air filled the cabin.

"Do you think it was sabotaged?"

"No, I think the dealer who sold it to me was a greedy, untrustworthy male—and I was a fool not to have examined it earlier. I'm going to see if I can determine what's wrong and see if there are any spare parts. But I'm not optimistic," he warned grimly as he climbed down.

She hesitated for a moment, then followed him. The pill had done its job and her headache had faded to no more than a dull ache. Her legs felt steadier too, and after a cautious few steps she walked around to the front of the flyer where Kalpar was giving the engine a disgusted look.

"Can you fix it?"

"I could—if I had a full workshop and several days to spend on it. I'm afraid we're going to have to walk, but it should only take a few days."

Days? In this wilderness? Her only previous exposure to nature had been a few trips to the park as a child. As an adult, she had attended several social events that had taken place at the botanical gardens, but she didn't think that counted. Her father's ruthlessly manicured roof garden certainly did not. Kalpar must have read her hesitant expression because his face softened.

"Don't worry, sweetheart. I'll take care of you."

"I know you will," she said honestly.

He sat back on his heels and looked up at the sky, already painted with the colors of dawn.

"If you feel up to it, we should probably get started. We can go as slowly as you need to and we can stop whenever you want, but I would feel more comfortable if we were away from the wreck. Vehicles can be tracked," he added at her confused look. "No one should be able to trace this back to me, but then I didn't think anyone could trace the warehouse back to me either."

"I don't mind walking," she said, shivering at the thought of being followed.

"Good. I'll get the bag and we'll get going."

She enjoyed the walk far more than she'd expected. Although the terrain could be a little rough, the fresh air and open sky lifted her spirits. After a lifetime cooped up in her father's sterile tower, the natural surroundings were a revelation. She found herself stopping constantly to touch the bark of an ancient tree, or run her fingers over a delicate blossom. Overhead, birds flitted through the canopy, trilling an exuberant song.

Kalpar made no attempt to rush her, allowing her to take her time and stop as frequently as she wished and doing his best to answer her eager questions. He possessed a surprising amount of knowledge about many of the plants they encountered.

Although he had seemed perfectly at home in Port Cantor, he moved just as easily through the wilderness.

"How do you know so much about all of this?" she asked when they stopped for a midday break in the shade of an enormous boulder.

"I grew up in a city so a new environment was... difficult at first. I decided the best way to handle it was to learn as much as I could. On Vizal, especially during the last years of the war, being able to survive in the wilderness was essential."

His face had turned grim, and she reached out to lightly touch his hand.

"I'm sorry you had to go through that."

"So am I, but perhaps it was the price I had to pay."

Pay for what, she wondered, but before she could ask, he went to collect water from a nearby stream. They rested a while longer, dozing in the warmth of the sun, then set off again. He kept the pace slow but steady, and by the time he decided they should make camp for the night, she thought they must have covered a considerable distance.

He had chosen a spot by another stream and she walked over to it to wash off the dust of travel, the water pleasantly cool after the heat of the day. By the time she returned, he already had a fire burning. He'd also placed a tarp on the ground between two large bushes and suspended another one over it to form a makeshift shelter. He went off to gather firewood, then made his own visit to the stream, returning with several good-sized fish. Watching him deftly clean and gut the fish with quick, precise movements filled her with admiration.

As he cooked the fish over the crackling fire, the smoky scent made her mouth water. She was suddenly ravenous after the long day of hiking and fresh air, waiting impatiently for the fish to cook. The simple fish turned out to be better than anything she'd ever tasted. He'd stuffed them with some wild greens that added a subtle citrus tang and she consumed every morsel.

"That was delicious," she said, unabashedly licking her fingers.

His eyes flared white as he watched her, but he shook his head.

"I suspect that hunger was the key ingredient."

"Maybe. I never really felt hungry at mealtimes—although I enjoyed eating a lot more once you joined me," she added shyly.

"A meal is always more pleasant with company."

After cleaning up, they returned from the stream to sit by the fire. She watched surreptitiously as the firelight played across his features, making them look both more alien and more attractive. In spite of everything, including his original plans for her, she was glad he was here. He made her feel safe in a way she'd never experienced. Impulsively, she leaned over and kissed his cheek.

"Thank you," she said softly, "for everything."

"How can you say that, now that you know what I was planning?"

Perhaps it was the uncertain light, but his face looked tired and strained.

"I understand that you were trying to protect your family. And whatever you may have planned, you've never done anything bad to me. You've watched over me, protected me, helped me escape." She gathered her courage and added softly, "And kissed me."

His eyes blazed white, but he shook his head.

"I shouldn't have done that."

"I wanted you to do it. I still do."

They stared at each other for a moment, and then he groaned and pulled her into his arms as his mouth descended over hers.

CHAPTER 12

Kalpar had replayed their kiss a thousand times in his head, but the memory was nothing compared to the reality of her delicious taste and shy enthusiasm. He tried to confine it to a simple kiss but when she tugged on his hair and tried to wiggle closer, he couldn't resist.

He slid his hand down to cup a small breast and brush his thumb across a stiff little nipple. She arched into his hand, silently seeking more, and he obliged, rolling the peak between his thumb and finger. Her body trembled, her small hands clutching desperately at his shoulders.

"That feels so... so..." she gasped.

"So good?" he asked, smiling at her innocent reaction.

"Y-yes," she whispered, her face flushed. "Good and achy and... needy. I don't know what to do."

"Let me show you, sweetheart."

He lowered his head to lick her nipple through her gown. When she shuddered and grabbed his head, he sucked hard and her hips bucked against him. He repeated the gesture, scraping his teeth gently across the stiff little bud, and she gave a soft cry. His cock jerked in response, the sensation unmistakable. It shouldn't be possible, but he couldn't deny his response to her.

He started to pull away but she clung to him, her blue eyes wide and dark in the firelight.

"Please don't stop. I want you to be the first to touch me. Everywhere."

How could he resist the earnest entreaty, a perfect match for his own increasing arousal? He leaned forward to suck on her other nipple, the satin gown adding to the delicious friction as she wiggled eagerly beneath him. He slid his hand down to cup her mound, the gown an unwelcome but necessary barrier between his hand and her soft skin. Her entire body jerked.

"Oh! It doesn't feel like that when I t-touch myself."

The memory of her hand buried between her legs flashed into his mind.

"Show me," he ordered, his voice rough.

She gave him an uncertain look, then shyly reached for the hem of her gown. He rewarded her with another hard pull on her nipple. As she drew the material up, he moved his hand so that he could watch the progress of the fabric. When the dress was gathered at her waist, he brought his fingers back to her exposed folds.

"You are so beautiful," he breathed.

She shivered under his touch, the smooth skin glistening with arousal. He brushed his thumb gently over her clit and her entire body convulsed. Her eyes flew open, her breath coming in frantic pants.

"It's... so much."

"Shhh, sweetheart, relax and enjoy it. I have you."

She took a deep breath and released it slowly, but she didn't try to get away. Instead, her hands closed on his shoulders again, gripping tightly as he resumed the slow strokes. Her entire body began to tremble and her eyes drifted shut.

"More," she pleaded.

She rocked her hips against him, seeking a firmer pressure. He smiled and rewarded her by dipping a single finger inside her impossibly tight channel. She cried out and he thrust shallowly, interspersing the thrusts with teasing brushes across her clit.

"Are you going to come for me, sweetheart?"

"Yes," she panted, her hands clutching at him frantically. "Yes. More. Please."

"Come for me, Constance. Come for me now."

He pressed firmly against her clit as he spoke and she immediately went rigid, her sheath clamping down on his fingers as she reached her climax. His cock responded as she cried out his name, swelling beneath his pants.

"K-Kalpar!"

He covered her mouth with his, kissing her fiercely until the tremors stopped and she collapsed against him with a sigh. He gathered her into his arms, her warmth and vulnerability threatening to overwhelm his remaining defenses.

When she yawned sleepily against his chest, he knew it was time to stop. He held her a moment longer, relishing the sweet weight of her in his arms, then rose carefully to his feet. Her eyes fluttered open as he carried her over to the temporary shelter he'd created. She sighed happily when he spread a thin thermal blanket over her, but she sat up again to watch as he banked the fire.

"Aren't you going to join me?"

The last thing he should do was to sleep with her, but how could he say no when she looked so sleepy and adorable? *And she said she trusted me*, he thought, remembering her words.

"Of course."

The shelter was too small for him to remain at a respectful distance but she didn't seem to mind, simply snuggling against his side. He automatically put his arm around her and she gave another happy sigh before falling asleep almost immediately. As soon as her breathing evened out, he reached down and grasped his cock, not fully erect but harder than he'd been since his youth.

He could no longer avoid the truth—this wasn't some type of hormonal imbalance—this delicate little female was his mate. The prospect filled him with joy. And terror. She deserved someone whole, someone not haunted by the past. He wasn't even sure their bodies were physically compatible, but it didn't seem to matter. She was his.

Now all he had to do was figure out how to keep his little mate safe.

The following morning they were surrounded by thick fog. He handed her a protein bar and she nibbled on it as they waited for the fog to clear. She kept stealing little glances at him from her lashes, a shy smile on her face. If they'd been in a more comfortable situation, he didn't think he would have been able to resist exploring more of her delicious little body.

"How long do you think it will take us to reach the farm?" she asked finally, her voice low and husky.

"Three days, I think. Maybe a little less if we increase our speed."

"No, don't do that," she said quickly, and he frowned down at her.

"Wouldn't you prefer sleeping in a comfortable bed in a house with a real kitchen?"

"I think I'd prefer last night."

Her obvious pleasure thrilled him, but it wasn't the original question. He reached over and pulled her onto his lap again.

"Do you not want to go to the farm?"

She played with the front of his shirt, avoiding his eyes.

"It sounds wonderful, but I started thinking... What if they don't like me because of my father?"

"His sins are not your fault."

"I know." She didn't look convinced. "But how can anyone welcome a c-criminal's daughter?"

"They welcomed me," he said quietly.

"Your father was a criminal? I don't believe it."

Bitterness flooded him and he had to fight the urge to growl at her.

"He was a thief. Not a particularly successful one, but he usually managed to steal enough to live on. He intended for me to follow in his footsteps. One of my earliest memories is of him hoisting me through a small window so that I could come around and unlock the door for him."

"That's terrible," she said indignantly, and her anger on his behalf helped ease the bitterness.

"Yes, but I doubt I would even have considered it wrong if he hadn't been confined for two years. I stayed with a distant relative during that time. Melaena was a formidable female but she had a kind heart beneath that fierce exterior and made it her job to teach me right from wrong."

"It obviously worked."

"Did it? I'm not always sure."

"I'm sure."

He tightened his arm around her, grateful for her support.

"My father wasn't happy when he returned and I started refusing to do everything he wanted me to do. He was determined to drag me back into it. And it wasn't just him. Almost everyone we knew was crooked in some way. I joined the military because it was the only way I could come up with to get away from that whole toxic environment. It was a good decision—up until Vizal."

Tired of dragging up the past, he rose to his feet and helped her up.

"I think the fog has cleared enough for us to continue."

She didn't argue, and the day continued much as the previous day had done. He enjoyed watching her innocent curiosity, happy to let her explore whatever they encountered. There was no rush to get to the farm, especially since he had nothing to report.

He pushed aside his feeling of guilt at that knowledge and focused on his mate instead.

Halfway through the afternoon they encountered a crystal clear pool with a small waterfall to one side and a sunny, moss-covered bank. Tiny purple flowers bloomed in the shady nooks next to the falls, releasing a sweet, heady fragrance.

"It's so beautiful," she whispered. "Can we stop and bathe in the pool?"

"It's likely to be cold," he warned, and she gave him a teasing look.

"Then you'll have to warm me up afterwards, won't you?"

His cock flexed again at the thought. It had remained in the same half-swollen state, unresponsive to his hand. He suspected it wouldn't respond to anything other than the touch of his mate. He could have sworn it grew a little more when she walked to the edge of the pool, shot him another sparkling look, then untied the makeshift sash and let her dress fall to the ground. Her cheeks turned pink, but she didn't shy away from his gaze, letting him watch her for a long moment before she stepped into the pool.

She shivered, her nipples pebbling from the cold, but she kept going, wading towards the falls. A drop of water ran down her back, tracing an intricate path down her spine. The drops of water sparkled in the sun, making him want to trace its path with his tongue. His cock flexed again.

"I was right," she said over her shoulder. "It feels wonderful, even if it is a little cold."

She bent down and scooped a handful of water, letting it pour through her fingers. He knew he should turn away. He should leave her here, walk away to a safe distance so that he could maintain control, but he couldn't tear himself away. She was his. He'd never believed that he would be able to have a true mate. The gods were offering him an unexpected gift and he couldn't refuse it.

"Take off your clothes and come join me," she called, her eyes daring him.

"Are you sure?" he growled.

She nodded.

"I'm sure. I want to see you again."

Hunger swept over him and he started undressing before she even finished her sentence. Her eyes widened as he removed his pants, but she didn't look away. He waded into the pool, ignoring the chill of the water and stalking towards her. The water was waist deep for him by the falls which meant it lapped around her pretty breasts and he couldn't resist tugging gently on a stiff little peak.

"Mmm, warmer already."

Despite her teasing words, her eyes were fixed on his cock, clearly visible in the clear water.

"You look… bigger," she said eventually, biting her lip.

"That's because I am. You have this effect on me."

He took her hand and guided it to his cock, groaning with pleasure as her warm little hand tried to close around him. Her eyes widened again as he grew a little larger.

"Does it just keep growing and growing?" she breathed, her thumb tracing one of the ridges along the side.

"No." Although right now it felt as if it did.

When she reached the head, it widened beneath her hand.

"For pleasure," he reminded her. "Wide enough to touch every part of you."

"Will it?" she whispered. "Will it touch every part of me?"

No. He should say no.

"Is that what you want?" he asked instead.

She looked up at him, studying his face, then gave a firm nod.

"Yes."

He was lost.

"Then let me touch you first."

The water lapped around their hips as he pulled her into his arms, pressing her breasts against his chest, and the water carried her scent to him. The primal aroma went straight to his brain, wiping out everything except his need for her. Her eyes grew dazed with need and she rubbed against him, the slickness of her sex evident, even in the water.

With a low groan, he cupped her bottom and lifted her against him.

"Wrap your legs around my waist."

Her legs tightened around him and he felt the slick wetness against his abdomen as well. It would be so easy to pull her up and drive into her. She would be so small and tight and - No.

Not like this. Not in the cold water, when he was on the verge of losing control. He wanted to take his time with her. He wanted to teach her to crave his touch the same way he craved hers.

When he turned to wade back to the shore, her eyes fluttered open.

"Where are you taking me?"

"Somewhere a little warmer," he promised, and he lifted her up into the sunlight, spreading her across the soft, mossy bank.

He licked a droplet of water off her breast, then sucked it into his mouth as her body arched. She whimpered but her hands dug into the moss. As he continued down her body, she spread her legs, allowing him to settle between them. His hands traced the delicate lines of her ribs, the curve of her hips, but he kept his mouth moving downwards.

She whimpered again as he gently parted her folds to reveal her tiny pearl, already pink and erect. He dropped a light kiss on it and she cried out, lifting her hips towards him. Another kiss and her legs shook. He closed his mouth over her, sucking gently. She cried out as she came, her hands clutching at his head.

"Perfect," he murmured, letting the word vibrate against the sensitive flesh.

As her shudders diminished, he began to kiss and lick the rest of her pretty pink folds, before pausing at the entrance to her core and slowly driving his tongue inside. Hot and tight and sweet. He stroked in and out until she was squirming then returned to her swollen clit. He licked and teased, building her passion again while he circled her entrance with one finger before slowly easing it into her tight channel. She arched against him as he sank it into her, crying out again, her sweet little sheath a velvet vice around his finger.

"More," she demanded.

"Such a demanding little mate."

Her eyes flew open.

"Mate?"

So much for his decision not to tell her. He distracted her by sucking her clit into his mouth again as he added a second finger. She came with a hoarse cry, her back bowing up from the ground.

"What do you mean? Mate?" she repeated breathlessly, as soon as she recovered.

"I'll explain later."

"You—"

Before she could protest, he began to rub a small circle around her clit with his thumb. Her words dissolved into a moan as he slid his fingers slowly in and out, the tip of one finger rubbing the slightly rougher patch of flesh behind her pubic bone.

"You will have to become used to your mate's touch," he whispered, and she came apart in his hands, her body straining, his name on her lips.

She was as ready as he could make her, and he positioned himself between her legs, stroking his cock through those slick, hot folds. The tip of his cock changed shape again to a smooth rounded point and he pressed it gently against her entrance. The first inch slid easily into that tight little passage, but then his cock widened and her body began to resist the intrusion. He swore, and she blinked up at him.

"S-so big."

He decided not to tell her he still wasn't completely erect, stroking a fingertip across her clit instead. Her hips jerked up at the contact and he slid a little deeper. Her eyes fluttered closed again as he continued to caress her. He rocked gently back and forth, his movement limited by the width of his cock. When her eyes opened and met his, he increased the pressure, taking advantage of her excitement to surge forward.

She whimpered as his cock continued to swell and he paused to check on her.

"More," she said, her eyes fever bright.

He pushed forward again, filling her to the limit, and her head fell back.

"Oh my. I feel so full."

He would have paused there but she wrapped her legs around his hips and tugged him closer, forcing him deeper and making them both groan. The pleasure threatened to overwhelm him as his fangs emerged. Clamping his lips together to avoid biting her, he began to move.

He fought to keep his movements gentle and steady, but she was too soft, too sweet, too arousing, and soon he was pounding into her, her soft cries urging him on. Her sheath gripped him so tightly that he could feel each rippling contraction as she came, and then he was coming with her, roaring out her name as the long years of emptiness disappeared, jet after jet of seed pumping into her willing body.

She was his.

CHAPTER 13

"Mate?" Constance asked again.

Kalpar sighed and finally looked up from where he was bathing her tender folds with a cool cloth.

"A bond between a male and a female."

A bond? Did he mean something similar to a marriage? Her heart skipped a beat.

"A permanent bond?" she asked carefully.

"It can vary from species to species." His eyes blazed white. "For the Catari it is permanent—but we were always taught that it would only exist between two Catari. And there is another component."

He parted his lips to reveal that his canine teeth had lengthened into small sharp fangs.

"You didn't have those before."

"No."

"Does that mean you want to… bite me?"

The thought sent a shiver down her spine but it was not entirely from fear, and his eyes dropped to her nipples as they stiffened at the thought. He ran his fingers lightly across the sensitive peaks, a thoughtful look on his face.

"This excites you?"

"I don't know," she said honestly. "Does it hurt?"

"It is supposed to enhance your pleasure, but of course I have no actual experience."

"Enhance it? I can't imagine it getting any better."

He chuckled and bent down to press a quick kiss to each breast. He sat back just as quickly and she pouted at him.

"Your body needs time to recover, sweetheart."

He was probably right—there was a definite ache between her legs. She sighed, and returned to the previous subject.

"So without the bite it's not a permanent mating?"

"Opinions differ." She was quite sure there was something he wasn't telling her but he gave her a final pat with the cloth and rose to his feet. "Shall we camp here tonight?"

"That sounds nice. It's so pretty."

"Beautiful," he agreed, but he was looking at her rather than their surroundings.

She blushed and sat up, reaching for her dress.

"I'd better get dressed. Otherwise you won't get anything else done today."

His low laugh sent a thrill of pleasure down her spine and she realized that she'd made him happy.

"I'm very tempted to take you up on that. But I want to set up camp before dark."

She nodded and pulled the dress over her head.

"Is there something I can do to help?"

"You can gather some of the smaller branches on the ground for use as kindling. The pond is too small for any large fish so I'm going to set a snare."

They both went to work, and by the time night fell they were sitting in front of the fire again as he turned two birds over the fire on a long branch. He had a pan of chopped tubers cooking below the birds and succulent juices dripped down into them. Although she'd averted her eyes while he prepared the birds, they smelled delicious and when he announced they were ready, she eagerly demolished her share of everything.

After they ate, she convinced him to tell her a little more about Catar and the female who had been such a major influence on him. He also told her some outrageous stories about his childhood escapades that she suspected were only half-true, but he kept her laughing until he decided it was time for bed. He carried her into their shelter and even though he refused to penetrate her, he used his mouth and hands until she was limp and happy and she fell asleep in his arms with a smile on her face.

The next morning she almost persuaded him to make love to her, but she couldn't hide a slight flinch when he tested her channel and he shook his head.

"This is like showing me a feast and then only letting me have one plate," she muttered, and he laughed.

"I promise you can feast tonight."

She smiled happily, then went to help break camp. After one last look at the lovely spot, they set out. The woods had thinned so they could see rolling hills beyond them but Kalpar decided to stick to the woods and their more abundant water sources. They stopped again at midafternoon in a pleasant little dell. He dropped the pack then caught her in his arms and kissed her until her knees went weak.

"I promised you a feast," he murmured, "and I intend to deliver as soon as we get everything set up—in case we're still feasting at nightfall."

"Sounds like a plan," she agreed breathlessly.

He gave her another quick kiss and went to gather wood. Her body hummed with anticipation, and she was so busy anticipating what was to come that the mocking voice caught her by surprise.

"Did you really think you could escape me?"

Her heart threatened to burst out of her chest as she whirled around to find Vexian standing behind her, flanked by two large, brutish humans. She looked around desperately, praying for the reassuring sight of Kalpar's tall purple figure. Instead, she saw his limp body half-hidden in the underbrush at the edge of the dell.

"Kalpar!"

She tried to go to him, but Vexian caught her wrist in his claw, not so careful with her this time. He looked even more terrifying in full daylight, the sun revealing the oily sheen to his skin. A sob caught in her throat but she refused to give him the satisfaction of her tears.

"W-what did you do to him?"

"For now I simply rendered him unconscious. I have more... interesting plans for him later. For both of you." He clicked his mandibles, his tongue flicking out. "I am really most disappointed that I am not to have the pleasure of breaking you in, but at least it means I won't have to be as careful with you."

"I don't want to marry you!"

"Oh, I'm afraid marriage is out of the question now. But your father assures me that you are still capable of bearing my clutch."

Bile filled her stomach, threatening to overflow.

"No..."

"Yes. I have already signed over my plebanium mines to him." He laughed. "He doesn't realize that they are worth very little, but then neither are you anymore."

"No," she whispered again, casting a despairing glance at Kalpar's position.

His body was no longer there.

She snatched her eyes away from the spot before Vexian could notice, her mind whirling. Had he regained consciousness and slipped away, abandoning her? *No.* He would never do such a thing. If he had left it was only so he could gain the upper hand against Vexian and his henchmen—which meant that she needed to keep him talking and distracted.

She lowered her head, doing her best to look limp and defeated.

"How did you find me?"

"I am tempted to say it is due to my superior intellect, but I'm afraid it is far more pedestrian. There is a tracking chip in the necklace you were wearing—the one you were foolish enough not to discard."

Her stomach churned. That must have been how her father's men had found the warehouse as well. How could she have been so stupid?

"And now, time for your first lesson."

As Vexian drew her inexorably towards him, she desperately scanned her surroundings, hoping for some sign of Kalpar. Where was he? What was taking so long?

Doubt tried to creep into her mind but she shoved it away. She had to believe Kalpar would come back for her. The alternative was too terrible to contemplate.

CHAPTER 14

Kalpar's head pounded as he came to, his vision slowly swimming back into focus as he blinked up at the trees overhead. Trees... For a moment he wasn't sure where he was or what had happened. Then it all came rushing back—the ambush, the blinding pain as something struck the back of his skull, and worst of all, Constance's panicked scream as Vexian's men descended on their camp.

Rage boiled up inside him—rage at Vexian and at her father but most of all at himself. He had failed her. After everything they had been through, he had let his guard down at the worst possible time. How could he have been so foolish? He'd learned long ago that a peaceful setting could conceal monstrous evil. Now she was at Vexian's mercy and it was his fault.

Gritting his teeth against the throbbing ache in his head, he forced himself to remain still as he took stock of the situation. He was lying in the brush at the edge of their camp, partially out of sight but still close enough to hear what was happening.

Turning his head in slow, almost imperceptible movements, he found a position where he could peer between the leaves. Constance was standing in front of Vexian, her eyes wide with fear as the Ctharan loomed over her. His stomach clenched as he saw her fragile wrist in his monstrous claw. The two henchmen were relaxed, leering at Vexian and Constance and clearly not expecting any more trouble. Amateurs.

His fingers twitched with the urge to draw his knives and charge, to rip the smug grin off Vexian's face, but he held himself in check. Although he was outnumbered, he was fast and he was accurate. Unfortunately, Vexian had Constance in his possession and that gave him the upper hand. For now. He couldn't risk her getting caught in the crossfire.

No, he would have to call on his former skills as a guerilla fighter, trained for stealth and precision strikes. If he could pick them off one by one he would stand a much better chance, and he decided the two henchmen were the easiest targets. They were complacent, not expecting an attack from the brush, and he would use that against them.

Slowly, carefully, he crept backwards through the undergrowth. As soon as he was out of sight of the camp, he circled around to approach from a different angle. As he moved he formulated a plan, visualizing the layout of the camp and calculating distances before creeping closer again.

As soon as he was in position, he drew his knives and crouched, poised and ready to strike. He picked up a small stone and tossed it next to the closest henchman's feet. As he expected, the man reflexively glanced towards the sound. As soon as he moved, Kalpar threw his knife. It embedded itself in the man's throat and he collapsed to the ground with no more than a quiet gurgle. Before the body even hit the ground, he was moving, slipping through the shadows beneath the trees towards the other henchman.

The fool hadn't even noticed that his partner had collapsed. He was fixated on Constance, a lustful leer on his face. Vexian was taunting her, but Kalpar slammed the door on his anger, forcing himself to stay calm and detached. Emotion would only make him careless.

He crept closer to the oblivious male using the natural camouflage of the forest until he was directly behind the hulking henchman. In one smooth motion, he slipped his knife across the man's throat. Dark blood spurted silently, but the body collapsed with a heavy thud.

Vexian whirled in shock at the noise, beady black eyes widening in alarm. He dropped Constance's arm as he turned, and Kalpar used the opportunity to attack. His knife sliced through the air, aiming straight for Vexian's heart, but the other male reacted with surprising speed, knocking his arm aside and deflecting the blow.

"You!" Vexian snarled in recognition.

Kalpar blocked out everything except the need to defeat this male and protect his mate. Without a word he struck again, feinting left before bringing his knife around in a deadly arc towards Vexian's ribs. The Ctharan barely managed to twist away, the blade leaving a long gash across his side, and he stumbled back with a howl of pain and outrage.

"I'll kill you for that!" he spat. "And then your female will pay for every mark!"

He didn't bother with threats or insults, circling warily. He feinted left, then right, watching for an opening. Vexian lashed out wildly with his claws, but he evaded the attack with ease.

"She is mine," Kalpar said finally, his voice deathly quiet. "You will not touch her."

Vexian roared and charged at him. At the last second, Kalpar dropped and rolled, coming up behind the Ctharan and driving his knife into the male's lower back with brutal force.

Vexian screamed in agony, crumpling to his knees as Kalpar wrenched the blade free. He pulled the male's head back and drew his knife across his throat in one brutal stroke, silencing Vexian's cries forever. Silence fell over the clearing. It was over. Their enemies were dead.

Chest heaving, he whirled around searching for Constance. She was pressed against a tree, her face pale but tears of relief in her eyes. She launched herself towards him but he reached her first, holding her close and breathing in her sweet scent. She sobbed against his chest and he closed his eyes in a grateful prayer. She was safe.

Now that the battle was over, his hands shook but it didn't matter. All that mattered was that his mate was in his arms where she belonged.

"I love you," he whispered, tightening his arm around her.

She looked up at him, tears still streaming down her cheeks as she gave him a radiant smile.

"I love you too."

His heart skipped a beat as he studied her face.

"Are you sure? Even though I was foolish enough to let down my guard and put you in danger?"

"Of course I'm sure! And you rescued me. Again."

"I will always rescue you," he promised.

"Hopefully you won't have to rescue me again," she said, and then she laughed and cried, but she was in his arms and that was all that mattered.

CHAPTER 15

Constance eventually pulled herself together enough to think about the future. She took a quick look at the three dead bodies and hastily looked away again. She didn't regret their deaths at all, but the sight of the bodies still made her queasy.

"What are we going to do about... them?"

"Nothing," he said calmly. "I will inform Commander Temel when we reach the farm and let him decide on the arrangements."

She breathed a sigh of relief.

"So we don't have to stay here?"

"Of course not." He hesitated for a second. "Vexian undoubtedly arrived by flyer, but I'd rather not take the chance that it was also tracked. Do you mind if we continue on foot and let Temel deal with that as well?"

"Not at all. I just want to get away from here because I want to celebrate our mating—and this isn't the most romantic place in the world."

He suddenly started to laugh, his expression lighter than he'd ever seen it.

"What's so funny?"

"A... friend of mine was in a similar situation and I didn't understand how he could be more focused on his mate than his dead enemies. Now I do. But I will follow my own advice and suggest we leave as quickly as possible. I would like to find another campsite before nightfall."

"As far away as possible," she said, the thought of being near the bodies after dark making her shudder.

"In that case, we best hurry." Despite his words, he didn't immediately release her. "I love you very much, my little mate. I'm sorry it took me so long to admit it."

She reached up to cup his cheek in her hand.

"Don't be sorry. I'm just glad that you finally figured it out."

He lowered his head and kissed her, his mouth demanding and possessive, as if establishing his claim, but all too quickly he pulled back with a rueful look.

"Supplies. Shelter. Then kissing."

"Hopefully a little more than kissing."

A little shocked by her own boldness, she brushed her hand across the front of his pants, delighted when his cock responded.

"Definitely more than kissing. Now stop distracting me."

He gave her another quick kiss then went to gather up their supplies. She didn't offer to help this time, keeping her back firmly to the campsite, afraid her stomach would rebel. He was still back at her side very quickly, tucking her under his arm as they left the clearing behind and she gave a sigh of relief.

He steered them towards the open fields alongside the woods. The sun was still high above the horizon and it all seemed so normal and peaceful that Vexian's intrusion already felt like a bad dream.

"I can't believe Vexian came after—Oh!" She came to a dead halt and frantically tried to grab the pack. "He said there was a tracking device in the necklace—that's how they found us."

He immediately removed the necklace and examined it, swearing when he located what looked like no more than a speck of white paint to her. He pried it off the necklace then crushed it between his nails.

"Civilian life has made me far too soft," he muttered. "I'm sorry, sweetheart."

"Stop apologizing. It didn't occur to me either." He still looked angry with himself, so she rubbed his cock again. "And I don't think you're too soft at all."

That surprised a laugh out of him and she felt inordinately pleased with herself.

He inspected the tiara and declared it tracker free, then hesitated.

"Would you rather we left these here?"

"Not unless you think it's necessary. They might come in useful in the future."

"Agreed."

He stuffed them back in the pack and they resumed their walk, keeping to the edge of the woods. They didn't encounter any streams, and she knew he was about to suggest that they go back into the woods when he spotted a structure in the distance.

"Look at that. I didn't realize we were this close."

"Close to what?"

"The farm."

She gave the dilapidated-looking barn a doubtful look.

"Really?"

"Well, part of it. This is one of the abandoned properties at the edge of the farm, but there should be a well and possibly even a roof."

"What luxury," she said dryly, and he laughed.

"We could go all the way to the main house, but it would require a few more hours of walking."

"No, this is fine. I'd rather be alone with you tonight anyway."

She was speaking the truth, but she was also still nervous about what the other people on the ranch would think of her.

His eyes flashed white and he started off again at a much faster pace as she laughed and tried to keep up.

When they reached the barn they discovered there was a house next to it as well, but it was in very poor shape. The paint was peeling off the barn and some of the boards were loose, but overall it was in better shape and they decided to spend the night there.

He wrestled open one of the big doors to let in some air, then went to get water from the well while she unpacked a few things. She pulled out a few protein bars and put them to one side, then took the tarp and spread it out across a couple of the ancient bales of hay. The hay gave off a sweet, musty smell as she removed her dress and perched there, waiting for him.

"I recognize this place now. We're further east than I thought. H'zim—"

His words died off as he saw her waiting for him. The heat rose in her cheeks, but she held out her hand to him.

"Come and join me."

He almost stumbled over his feet in his haste to do so, and she giggled.

"I don't think we need the water yet."

He looked down at the bucket as if he'd forgotten it was there, then smiled and put it down.

"You are an extraordinarily distracting female."

"Good. Now take off your clothes and come here."

"Yes, ma'am."

As soon as he stripped off his clothes, his cock rose, long and thick between them, and she gulped. It was almost impossible to believe that her body had been able to take that thick purple shaft. *But it did, and it was wonderful,* she reminded herself.

He put a casual hand on his cock, stroking his fingers along the ridges as he stalked towards her.

"You are a miracle, my little mate. I never thought to experience this again." She bit her lip as he reached her and he gently cupped her face. "I would not have wanted to experience it with anyone else."

"Really?"

"Really."

He leaned down and kissed her, his cock nudging against her belly as she opened for him. His big body surrounded her, filling her senses and blocking out everything else. She was already hot and wet and eager, her clit pulsing with excitement, but he took his time, leisurely exploring her mouth while his hands roamed over her body, dancing across her skin but not lingering.

By the time he reached her nipples, she was desperate for his touch. He teased the erect points, gently rolling them between his fingers. She arched against him, silently asking for more, and he finally obliged by moving to her thighs and spreading them apart to cup her mound.

She moaned as he traced the outside of her folds, her entire body quivering with need. He continued to tease her, his thumb brushing over her clit but not making direct contact as he slid a finger inside her channel. When he finally pressed against her clit, she came with a strangled cry, her sheath spasming around his finger.

He purred approvingly, his mouth ghosting down over her neck to linger in the sensitive spot where it met the curve of her shoulder.

"Are you going to bite me?" she asked breathlessly.

He froze, then raised his head so he could watch her face.

"Is that what you want?"

"Yes," she said firmly.

He stroked his thumb over the soft skin.

"You understand that the bond is forever?"

"As far as I'm concerned it already is."

He shuddered, then pressed his lips to her neck again, licking and sucking—but not biting—and she gave him a puzzled look when he raised his head again.

"You didn't do it? Did you change your mind?"

"No, my little mate, but it isn't time yet. I won't sink my fangs into you until I'm buried deep in your sweet little cunt." Her mouth dropped open, and he laughed. "But first I will prepare you."

"I'm prepared," she protested, trying to pull him closer, but he only laughed again as his clever fingers teased her nipples.

"Maybe so, but I'm not. And I want to explore every inch of your pretty body."

"I—Oh my."

He replaced his fingers with his mouth, sucking in her nipple, and her body ignited all over again. She squirmed helplessly as he nipped and licked his way between her breasts, his hands kneading and stroking in turn, drawing the pleasure out for endless minutes before turning his attention to the other side. By the time he finished, she was practically writhing, but he still wasn't done.

He kneeled before her, his mouth hovering just above her slit. He didn't touch her with anything but his breath.

"So pink and pretty and soft," he murmured, and she shivered as the light touch caressed her.

His tongue darted out to taste her, the tip just tracing over her clit, and her hips jerked as she whimpered for more. He growled approvingly and did it again. And again. Long, slow licks, back and forth over her flesh, making her moan and wiggle, but not giving her the pressure she craved. Her hands tightened in his hair as she tried to drag him closer but he remained infuriatingly out of reach.

"Please."

"Tell me what you need, my little mate."

"You. I need you."

"Need me where?"

"Inside me," she gasped.

He pressed his nose against her, inhaling deeply.

"Here?"

He drove a finger deep inside her, pumping slowly in and out and she squirmed on the digit.

"No. More."

"I will give you more," he promised.

He added a second finger and her pussy clenched around it.

"More."

"Like this?"

He licked her again, adding just the slightest flick of his tongue and she groaned in frustration.

"That's not what I want."

"Are you sure?"

"Yes. Yes, I'm sure. Please."

He made a deep humming noise and then his mouth was on her, sucking gently as he pushed another finger inside her and she exploded in pleasure. She was still quivering when he placed her on her hands and knees on the bale in front of him, his cock sliding easily through her slick folds and nudging her still swollen clit with each stroke.

"Do you think you're prepared now?"

"God, yes."

The words barely escaped before he drove into her in one long hard stroke. He'd never taken her so forcefully before, embedding himself so deeply. Her pussy fluttered wildly around him as the tip of his cock changed shape, widening until it dragged over every inch of her channel as he slowly withdrew, then thrust back in just as hard, sending her flying as she clutched desperately at the straw. He grabbed hold of her hips, his big hands almost spanning them as he held her in place for thrust after thrust.

Her climaxes rolled on and on, and each time she started to come down he'd make some minor adjustment and send her flying all over again. He started to speed up, losing his careful rhythm as he bent down over her back, his mouth unerringly finding that place on her neck.

"I claim you as my mate, Constance. For now. Forever."

Then his fangs sank into her neck.

Her vision sheeted white as pure, primitive pleasure blasted through her body, her climax hitting her like a tsunami, sweeping her down and under in dizzying circles. His cock grew until she was so full she couldn't breathe and he finally came with a triumphant roar, jet after jet of seed flooding her body, the rush of heat adding to the sensations overwhelming her, the force of her final orgasm shaking her to the core.

Then he wrapped his arms around her and rolled so that they were lying on their sides, her back tight to his front, his cock still deep inside her as he licked her neck, soothing the sting, even that gentle touch making her shiver.

"Is it possible to die from pleasure?' she asked, only half-joking.

He laughed, the vibration sending another quiver of excitement through her body.

"I don't believe so, but we can certainly test that theory."

"You got bigger," she accused.

"Yes. The mating bite is the final piece."

"So you won't get any bigger?"

He laughed again and nuzzled her bite mark.

"Are you disappointed?"

"No. I'm just trying to figure out if I'll ever be able to walk again."

"If you can't, I'll carry you," he promised.

"Deal."

They lay there together for a long time. Her mind drifted in lazy contented circles as an early evening breeze swept through the barn carrying the scent of flowers and sun-warmed earth. Through the open barn doors she could see the sky beginning to darken, color streaking the horizon as a few low clouds floated across the sky.

Then a hulking figure filled the opening and she bit back a scream. Kalpar immediately tensed and crouched in front of her, reaching for the knives he'd abandoned while she pulled the tarp around her body.

"What the fuck are you doing here?" the figure demanded, and Kalpar straightened.

"Godsdammit, H'zim, you almost got a knife through your heart."

"No, I didn't. You were too busy mating to pay attention."

Kalpar's voice turned low and dangerous.

"How long have you been here?"

"Too long. I was looking for—" H'zim took a step closer and now that he was no longer silhouetted against the sun, she could see he had a terrifyingly hard face, his green skin marked with scars. "It's none of your fucking business. I want to know why you're here. No one is supposed to fucking bother me."

"Then stay on your own fucking farm," Kalpar snapped. "You don't own this whole sector."

"Are you moving in?"

"No, but I could."

"I don't fucking like it."

"Then go back to your own damn farm."

H'zim gave him a fearsome glare, then turned around and stomped out. It wasn't until Kalpar turned back to her that she suddenly noticed that he was still completely naked—not that either male seemed to care.

"Someone you know, I take it?" she asked, trying not to giggle.

"Unfortunately." He sighed and sat down next to her. "That's not fair. He's a former member of our squad as well, but he served several years in jail on a trumped-up charge and now he's angry at the world. Well, angrier. He's never been what I would call happy."

"He lives out here? By himself?"

"Yes, he took the most remote farm—although he now seems to think that includes all of the surrounding territory as well. I'll talk to the Commander and his brother S'kal about it tomorrow. Sorry, sweetheart. I know he ruined the mood."

She shrugged, smiling as he immediately focused on her breasts.

"Still better than dead bodies," she said firmly. "Can I have some water, please?"

He looked down, then groaned.

"Sorry. I knocked it over when I jumped up."

"That's all right. I'll go get some more—wearing my dress."

"Probably just as well, but I can do it."

"Why don't you see if you can figure out something for dinner other than protein bars? I have a feeling I'll need to keep my strength up."

"I'll see what I can find."

She gave him a quick kiss, then pulled on her dress and went to refill the bucket of water. After she pulled it up, she paused for a moment, looking around at the rapidly darkening landscape. A flash of yellow in the nearby woods caught her attention.

Curious, she took a few steps towards the woods and came face to face with another woman. The stranger appeared to be around her age and was about the same height, but the resemblance ended there. The other woman had curves for days and an impish, pixie-like face, not to mention flaming red hair and freckles covering every inch of exposed skin.

They stared at each other, then the woman gave her a mischievous look and put her finger over her lips before disappearing back into the woods. For someone with such vivid coloring, she disappeared extraordinarily quickly, leaving Constance staring into the woods wondering if she'd imagined the whole encounter.

Perhaps she had, she decided, returning to the barn and immediately forgetting about everything except her new mate.

CHAPTER 16

Constance tugged nervously at her dress, wishing it wasn't quite so worn from their adventures. She would have almost preferred to be wearing one of her old long-sleeved high-neck dresses. *No, I wouldn't,* she told herself firmly. That life was behind her now.

"Stop fidgeting," Kalpar said, squeezing her hand. "You look beautiful."

"No, I don't, but thank you."

"You do to me," he said firmly. "And you have no reason to be nervous."

"What if everyone hates me because of my father?"

"They won't."

His confidence helped soothe her fears a little as they walked down the road towards the main farmhouse. It was a stunning contrast to the abandoned farm where they'd spent the night.

Everything looked prosperous and well-cared for, from the big white farmhouse to the outbuildings to the fields full of grain.

"It all looks so beautiful and peaceful, but I have no idea why my father would be interested."

"Unfortunately, neither do we."

"I'm sorry your plan didn't work out."

He shrugged. "As much as I want to know what's going on, finding you was far more important."

"Thank goodness you did."

They turned into the driveway leading up to the big farm house, but they hadn't reached it when an older woman came rushing out. She was pretty and plump and gave them both a welcoming smile.

"It *is* you, Kalpar. I didn't believe it when Tomlin told me you were coming although I should have known better. And who is this?"

"Ida, this is my mate, Constance."

Ida beamed at her.

"I'm delighted to meet you, Constance."

She tentatively returned Ida's smile, then took a deep breath. She was determined to be honest with everyone from the beginning.

"My full name is Constance Thompson."

"Thompson? You mean like…"

"Like Marshall Thompson? Yes. He's my father."

"Oh, you poor child." Ida gave her a quick impulsive hug, and she suddenly had to fight back the tears. "I'm sure you're going to be much happier here."

Kalpar was giving her a "told you so" smile over Ida's head but she ignored him and gave the other woman a watery smile.

"I know I will be."

"Of course, you will. Now come on back to the kitchen. I'm sure you must be hungry after your journey... You didn't walk all the way from Port Cantor, did you?"

"No, our flyer crashed. If you don't mind, Ida, we need to talk to Temel before we do anything else."

Ida shook her head and gave Constance a rueful grin.

"Of course you do. One of these days someone will show up and just want to visit and I'll faint from shock." She shepherded them into the house, then squeezed Constance's hand. "I'll be in the kitchen if you need me. Temel is in his study as usual."

Kalpar nodded, then put a hand on her back and escorted her through a set of double doors to a large book-lined study with a wide picture window looking out over the property. Two men were standing at the desk, looking over a set of plans. One of them was an alien—a large blue-skinned male with sweeping horns. He had a stern face and an air of command but he gave them both a warm smile. The other man was human, tall and lean with short dark hair, and was dressed all in black. He nodded calmly at both of them. Neither male seemed surprised to see them.

Kalpar straightened into a military posture.

"I regret to report, Commander, that my mission was a failure."

"It doesn't appear to have been." Temel smiled at her again. "I hear that the two of you are mated."

How could he have known? She gave Kalpar a puzzled look, but he just shook his head.

"This is my mate, Constance. Constance, this is Commander Temel and Tomlin."

"Constance Thompson," she added firmly, but Temel's expression didn't change.

He nodded thoughtfully.

"A much more desirable outcome than a kidnapping."

"You knew about that?"

"It is more accurate to say we suspected," Tomlin said calmly.

"I'm very happy with the outcome, but I'm sorry I didn't discover anything useful."

"There is one thing," she said slowly. "I'm not sure it's useful, but it's unusual enough that maybe it matters?"

Tomlin looked at her. He had the polished dignity of a valued servant, but she'd been surrounded by servants all her life and she was quite sure he wasn't a servant.

"Please go on."

"My father was negotiating for me to be m-married to Lord Vexian."

Something unreadable flashed across Tomlin's face, but he didn't comment.

"I assumed it was to expand his holdings, but Vexian told me that after I was… sullied, my father traded me for some mining property that Vexian said was useless."

By the time she'd finished, her face was red with embarrassment but she'd managed to get it all out. Kalpar put a comforting arm around her shoulders and she leaned gratefully against his side.

"What kind of mines?" Tomlin asked, his voice a fraction less calm.

"P something. Pla—no, plebanium."

"Interesting," Tomlin murmured, but once again she had the impression he wasn't quite as calm as he'd appeared before.

"Does that mean something to you, Tomlin?" Temel asked.

"Perhaps, Lord Temel. Not by itself, but in combination..."

Since Tomlin was clearly lost in his own thoughts, Temel turned back to them.

"Have you discussed living arrangements?"

"Not really. I thought we would continue to stay in the bunkhouse for a while and then Constance could decide where she would like to live."

"Good. It will be nice to have you close at hand again."

"Is Celenk tired of being the only one looking after the cattle?" Kalpar said dryly, and Temel laughed.

"I doubt he would admit it, but I'm sure he will be happy you're back. Now why don't we join my mate in the kitchen?"

As they all headed out of the office, Tomlin suddenly stopped, his head swiveling over to the pack that Kalpar had left lying by the door.

"What do you have in your pack, Lord Kalpar?"

"The usual—survival equipment, food, and other supplies. It's a standard bag."

"Nothing else?"

There was a hint of urgency beneath the calm voice, and she gave him a puzzled frown.

"Do you mean the jewelry?"

"What kind of jewelry?"

Kalpar looked at her and she shrugged so he bent over and pulled out the necklace and tiara. Tomlin didn't try and take them—just gave them a thoughtful look.

"Would it be possible to borrow them? They will be safe with me."

"I suppose so—but why?" she asked.

"It may prove useful to my investigation. Am I correct in assuming that your father gave them to you?"

It was a logical assumption, but once again she had the impression there was something else behind it.

"Yes, he did. There was a tracker on the necklace but we destroyed it."

"Yes, they're clean. Would you mind placing them on the desk, Lord Kalpar?"

Her mate frowned but obeyed, and then the four of them resumed their journey to the kitchen.

. . .

Several hours later, Kalpar swung her hand as they walked down a flower-lined trail to his bunkhouse.

"Tired, sweetheart?"

"A little. It's just... a lot of people."

It seemed silly to say that given the number of times she'd attended functions with hundreds of people, but she'd always felt as if she were in her own private bubble for those events and in between them she was usually alone. The males and mates and children who had joined them in the kitchen had seemed genuinely interested in her, and even though all of them were very nice, she'd found it rather overwhelming. She was happy it was just the two of them again.

"You'll get used to it."

"I know, and I'm sure I'll enjoy it eventually. But you'll have to remind me who everyone is."

Other than the original three people, the only one who stood out was a reptilian alien with orange and gold scales and a tail. He and Kalpar had exchanged a number of barbed comments, but she'd finally decided they were actually friends.

The bunkhouse was a long low building with a porch across the front and she expected to find a utilitarian interior. Instead, he opened the door to reveal a large living area with an extremely well-equipped kitchen at one end. Comfortable furniture was arranged around a big stone fireplace, and she could see a large bedroom through the door next to it.

"This is the bunkhouse?" she asked, turning to take it all in.

"Originally, yes, and there is a room with a set of four bunks behind the pantry, but I'm much too large to sleep in a bunk.

Once I decided to build a bedroom, it just escalated. What do you think?"

"I love it." She walked over to the wall of windows opposite the porch that looked out over the farm and sighed happily. "It feels… it feels like home."

"It is your home now—unless you'd rather move out on to one of the farms?"

"And become H'zim's neighbor?"

She grinned at him and he grinned back, even though he shook his head.

"There are other options."

"I think we'll be happy right here. Although maybe we should do one thing—just to make sure."

"What's that?"

"Test out the bed."

His eyes flared white and then he was carrying her through into the bedroom.

"We'll conduct a very thorough test," he promised.

The test was very thorough indeed, but the results were absolutely conclusive—the bed was perfect, the house was perfect, and he was perfect. She was home at last.

CHAPTER 17

alpar landed the flyer at an obscure landing field that didn't feel the need to register arrivals and departures. He paid the modestly exorbitant fee for that privacy, then made his way quietly to Thompson Tower. As he had suspected previously, the underground garage was almost laughably easy to infiltrate, especially since he knew exactly which areas the monitors covered.

Once he was inside, it was simply a matter of concealing himself and waiting. The first time Marshall came out, he was accompanied by three other men, and Kalpar reluctantly decided it wasn't worth the stir it would cause to take on all three of them. He settled back to wait for another opportunity.

It came later that night when Marshall returned alone.

He waited until the other male dismissed his driver, then came up behind him and put his knife to his throat as he drew him back into the shadows. Marshall froze as the blade touched his throat, but when he spoke his voice was as calm and icy as ever.

"What do you want?"

"To provide you with two pieces of information. First, Vexian is dead."

"I agree that is an interesting piece of news," Marshall said slowly. "It could prove very useful. But since a knife seems unnecessary for the delivery of such a message, what is the second piece of information?"

"Your daughter is no longer a bargaining tool."

Even this close to the other man, Kalpar couldn't detect any visible reaction to his statement.

"That is unfortunate, but hardly news. I assumed it would be the case as soon as she left my protection."

Protection? He let his knife draw a thin line of blood.

"She is much better off without your so-called protection. I just want you to understand that she is of no further interest to you."

After the slightest pause, Marshall shrugged.

"With Vexian dead you are correct that I have no use for her. No current use, anyway. Especially if she is no longer... intact."

His knife pressed a little deeper.

"No current or future use," he warned.

"On one condition."

The man thought he could negotiate with a knife at his throat? He might be a despicable bastard, but he had courage.

"This is a mutual arrangement," Marshall continued. "She is not to expect anything from me—"

"She does not want anything you have to offer," he growled.

"And she is to take no interest in my business. The organizations with which she was involved have been informed that she has gone offworld for health reasons." His voice turned even colder. "I trust nothing will occur to contradict that story."

"It will not."

After a brief hesitation, Marshall said slowly, "You do realize she is still my heir?"

It hadn't occurred to him, but Constance had told him she didn't have any other family, and Marshall certainly didn't have any friends. Not that it made any difference.

"She's not interested."

"After living in squalor for a few years that may change. You may tell her that I would be willing to... discuss such matters in the future."

He wanted to snarl that she would never be interested in anything the man had to offer, but he reluctantly decided that he would at least pass on the message.

"Fine. That concludes our business."

He let the knife drop and faded back into the shadows. Marshall didn't even look around. He reached into his pocket and pulled out a handkerchief, dabbing delicately at the thin line of blood before continuing to the elevator bank as if nothing had happened.

Kalpar watched him go, hoping he hadn't made a mistake in leaving him alive. He didn't trust the man for a minute, but he did believe that Marshall was motivated purely by self-interest. If he had decided that Constance was of no further use to him, he had no reason to pursue her. The fact that he had not bothered to search for her lent credence to that assumption.

He slipped back out of the garage and returned to his flyer. He reached the farm just as the sun was rising. Somewhat ironically, the flyer was the same one Vexian had used to follow them. Tomlin had made sure the original tracking device was removed, then wiped the data. Kalpar did the same for the current trip, then programmed an erratic flight pattern that would eventually take the flyer to one of his contacts and sent it on its way before hurrying back to his house.

Constance was asleep on the couch and he suspected she'd fallen asleep waiting for him. She looked so pretty and innocent in her sleep that he didn't have the heart to wake her. He bent over, intending to carry her to their bed, but as soon as he touched her, her eyes flew open.

"You're back!" She gave him a quick, anxious look, then wrapped her arms around his neck with a relieved sigh. "Did everything go all right?"

He smiled and sat down on the couch, pulling her onto his lap.

"Yes. I delivered the message. Your father appears to have accepted that you are out of his reach."

"You didn't have to... hurt him?"

The hint of anxiety on her face was the other reason he had let Marshall live. Although she claimed to be uninterested in her father's fate, he didn't entirely believe her.

"He was fine when I left," he assured her.

The almost imperceptible sigh of relief confirmed his suspicions.

"Do you really think he will leave us alone?"

"I... hope so. If nothing else, I believe he will be occupied taking over as much as possible of Vexian's empire."

"Too occupied to worry about the farm?"

He wasn't quite as sure about that, but he kept his doubts to himself.

"I believe so, but we will continue to work on improving our security."

She nodded thoughtfully, accepting his words, and then her small hand stroked a teasing line down his shirt.

"I missed you last night. I don't like sleeping without you."

The first real smile tugged at his lips.

"I can assure you that it is something you will never have to do again. I missed you as well."

She looked up at him, her eyes gleaming.

"Why don't you show me how much?"

His cock jumped at the invitation in her voice, but he forced himself to speak in a stern tone.

"You need your rest."

"Don't you want to help me sleep?"

He fought to keep his face stern, but his cock had already made its choice and it was growing rapidly as she wriggled her little bottom against it.

"Very well. Merely to make you sleep well."

"Of course," she said innocently.

He laughed, then rose with her in his arms and carried her into the bedroom. He laid her gently down on the bed and undressed her slowly, letting his hands linger on every inch of newly exposed skin. She tried to speed up the process by tugging at his clothes, but he caught her hands and pulled them above her head.

"No. I intend to savor this."

She gave him a playful pout and he lowered his head to kiss her, licking gently at the seam of her lips. She opened eagerly, her small tongue dancing against his as he explored her slowly. He nipped lightly at her plump lower lip and her hips arched off of the mattress as she whimpered against his lips.

"Kalpar. Please."

He trailed kisses down her throat and took his time tasting the silky skin of her neck. When he reached her mating bite, he lingered, sucking hard. She shivered in response, her body writhing beneath his.

"More."

He obliged her, licking and nipping his way down to her breasts. They were so soft and delicate he tried to restrain himself but she urged him on impatiently. He used his tongue to caress one tender nipple, and she moaned as he switched to the other one. He moved his hand to her neglected breast, rolling the peak between his thumb and forefinger and tightening his grip as she arched against him. He returned to her mouth, kissing her with all the passion he'd been holding back, and she returned the kiss just as enthusiastically, her mouth eager and demanding.

He left her long enough to tear off his own clothing, then stood for a moment admiring the delightful picture she presented. Her pretty lips were pink and swollen, the exact same shade as her stiff little nipples, and even her mating bite glowed pink against her flawless skin. When he bent down and brushed his fingers along her delicate folds, he found her hot and wet. When he pressed the tip of his finger inside her, she gasped but he found no resistance and he added a second finger.

"That feels so good," she whispered, rocking against his fingers as a tide of pink spread from her cheeks down to her pretty breasts.

He sank to his knees next to the bed, his face level with her sex. As he slid his fingers gently in and out, he put his mouth over her and drew her swollen clit into his mouth.

She cried out, her hips arching and he continued his steady assault, stroking her with his fingers as his tongue stroked her little bud. The scent and taste of her intoxicated him and he would have been perfectly happy to spend hours devoting himself to her pleasure, but she began to shudder and cry out, her small fists clenching in the sheets and her body quivering.

He suckled harder, fingers curling and twisting until she came, calling out his name in a low, hoarse cry. Her climax was sweet and lush, and he kept up his stimulation until she was lying limply on the mattress. Her eyes were heavy with pleasure as she watched him bring his fingers to his lips and lick them clean.

"Delicious."

Her face flushed adorably, but a satisfied smile curved her lips.

"Can I do that to you?" she asked shyly.

"Not today," he said firmly, stroking his throbbing shaft. "This time I need to be inside you."

She gave a happy little sigh and parted her thighs in silent invitation, the tempting sight impossible to resist. He braced himself over her as he captured her mouth again, then placed the head of his cock at her entrance. The head had already assumed the pointed shape designed for penetration and she took the tip easily enough.

He still had to work the rest of his shaft inside her, but she was hot and slick from her climax and she adjusted to his size as if she'd been made just for him. Her channel gripped him so tightly that he tried to restrain himself, to give her more time to adjust, but she moved frantically against him, sweet little cries falling from her lips and he could hold back no longer. He surged deep, filling her again and again as she cried out in pleasure.

"Yes, yes, like that. More," she demanded and he happily complied, driving into her over and over again.

Her body began to quiver, her inner walls clutching at him as she cried out his name and he roared as his own climax shook him, pleasure sweeping through his entire body.

As the last ripples died away, he gathered her close, cuddling her against his chest as he fought to catch his breath. No one was ever going to take her away from him. He would guard her and keep her safe for the rest of her life.

"I love you," she whispered, lifting her face to his.

"I love you too, sweetheart."

She gave him a beaming smile and he wrapped his arms around her, marveling at the unexpected gift he had found. She had filled a void in his soul that he'd believed would remain empty forever, and he would always be grateful.

EPILOGUE

 our months later...

KALPAR HURRIED INTO HIS OFFICE AND SCATTERED CATTLE breeding records across his desk. By the time Constance came dancing in a few moments later, he looked as if he'd been working all morning. He had not. She'd spent the last month working on Christmas presents for the children in the hospital in Port Cantor. The project had somehow grown to include most of the women on the ranch as well as several in Wainwright, the nearest small town, but she managed it with the same efficiency she'd managed her previous charity work.

This morning she and Ida had gone into Wainwright to meet with the women in town and arrange for the presents to be transported to Port Cantor anonymously. When he'd offered to take her, she'd refused, assuring him she could handle the trip. He'd wanted to insist, but he knew how important her new freedom was to her. Only his determination never to remind her of her father had enabled him to rein in his protective instincts where she was concerned. Mostly.

He'd satisfied that need to protect her by following at a discreet distance, remaining out of sight as she went about her business. She already knew almost everyone in town and greeted them cheerfully. Without the specter of her father behind her, she received genuinely friendly responses, and although he would rather have been at her side, he enjoyed watching her happiness.

Now he held out his hand and she came to him immediately, hopping onto his lap with an excited bounce.

"Did you enjoy your trip to town?"

"I did. We're going to work on a second set of presents for the local children, and we've already started talking about what else we can do to help. It's nice to know I can be useful even without the money."

"Of course you can."

"And then on the way back it started snowing!"

"I can see that," he said gravely, brushing away the white flakes still caught in her long blonde curls. "But you can't tell me that you've never seen snow before."

"Occasionally. From the penthouse, but city snow isn't the same." A shadow crossed her face at the reminder and he tugged her closer. "Did you enjoy the snow?" she added, giving him an innocent look.

"I like snow," he said cautiously, and she giggled.

"Just as well, since you were on horseback and not in a carriage."

"You knew?"

"Of course I knew." She leaned in and brushed her cold little lips against his. "But thank you for trying to let me think I was going by myself."

"I worry." He ran his finger across her lower lip. "You must be careful not to allow yourself to get wet and chilled."

She rolled her eyes at him.

"I'm not as fragile as you seem to think."

"You can still get cold." He slipped his hand into her open jacket and cupped a small breast, brushing his thumb across the erect tip. "Are you sure you aren't chilled?"

"I-I don't know." She shivered as he repeated the caress, her eyelashes fluttering down. "Maybe I do need a little warming up."

He laughed softly as he tugged her against him, his mouth lowering to hers. He intended the kiss to be no more than a quick caress to satisfy his need to reassure himself that she was truly his, but she whimpered and pressed against him, her mouth opening beneath his, inviting him to taste her.

Groaning, he took her mouth more thoroughly, drinking in her sweetness as his hands roamed over her slender body. When he finally lifted his mouth from hers, she was panting.

"I'm much warmer now," she whispered, struggling out of her jacket.

The soft sweater she was wearing beneath it clung lovingly to her delicious little body, and she wiggled happily as he plucked at one of those impudent nipples.

"Are you sure?" he asked, nuzzling the delicate curve of her neck.

"Not quite."

"Hmm. Well, we'll just have to see if I can do something to help."

He lifted her from his lap, placing her on the edge of his desk and spreading her legs so that he could settle between them. A tiny shiver trembled through her body, but she raised her arms willingly as he lifted her sweater over her head, exposing her pretty breasts to his avid gaze.

He groaned and leaned forward to suck one tight nipple into his mouth.

"Oh. That's nice. I… Oh my goodness."

His mouth and fingers teased her delicate little breasts until she was writhing on the edge of the desk.

"Hold on," he ordered, putting her arms around his neck.

She obeyed eagerly as he lifted her high enough to strip away her jeans, leaving her in nothing but a tiny scrap of blue lace.

"Very pretty," he said approvingly, tugging on the fabric so it slid across her already swollen clit. "Are they new?"

"Y-yes."

He tugged a little harder and her whole body quivered.

"I will allow you to keep them on," he decided as he rose to his feet and freed his erection, "for now."

"What do you—"

Her words died in her throat as he slid two fingers beneath the band and found her slick little cunt. He traced along the damp folds, then circled her clit. Her back arched at the contact, offering her breasts to him again, and he obligingly bent down to draw one tightly puckered peak into his mouth, his fingers never stopping their caresses. She squirmed against his hand, her little moans sending jolts of electricity straight to his cock.

He straightened up abruptly, closing his fist around the base of his erection and squeezing hard. His other hand fumbled in the drawer next to her hip as he stared down at her, desperate to drive his aching cock into her silken heat. With her eyes closed, she didn't notice him lifting the small bottle out of the drawer until he dropped several cool drops on her heated flesh.

"What's that?" she asked as he also coated his fingers.

"Something to enhance your pleasure."

Her eyes widened as he slid two well-greased fingers into her, and he cupped her cheek with his other hand as the oil began to work.

"Oh! That feels all warm inside."

She squirmed against his hand as he stroked slowly in and out.

"I told you I didn't want you to get chilled."

"Yes, but—"

She broke off on a gasp as his thumb circled her clit again and her nails dug into his shoulders.

"Kalpar!"

He loved hearing her cry out his name, and he rewarded her by pressing another finger into her tight entrance.

"Push against me."

Her eyes widened again, but she obeyed, and the combination of the extra stretching and the stimulation of her clit sent her over the edge. Her cries filled the room as she jerked against his fingers, her orgasm a sweet torture to his own throbbing cock. As soon as her tremors started to slow, he withdrew his hand. Pulling the strip of lace to one side, he positioned the tip of his shaft against her entrance, just as he had so many times before.

His cock tingled from the heated oil but he waited until her eyes opened. She looked so tiny, so innocent, but her smile was slow and sensual.

"Ready, sweetheart?" he asked roughly.

She nodded, her face flushed with desire, and he drove home in one hard thrust. She cried out, her slick channel convulsing around him again, and he was lost.

"Yes," he groaned, thrusting deep.

Over and over, again and again.

Her second climax was even stronger than the first and he rode it out, his cock filling her completely as she cried out his name. One more stroke. Two, and then he came with a roar, her muscles rippling around his rigid shaft, milking him of every drop.

"Now are you warm enough?" he teased, once he could speak again.

"As long as you love me, I'll always be warm enough."

A warm glow filled his own chest as he smiled down at her.

"In that case, you'll never be cold."

He gently pulled free, then sat back in his chair and tucked her against him, completely content.

"Did you pay attention to everywhere I went?" she asked, stroking his chest.

"Of course. Why?"

"Then you saw that Ida and I went to visit Sara."

Her voice was so casual that he gave her a suspicious look.

"I know. She's one of the women who is making presents."

"Mmhmm." She ran her fingers down his chest again. "Do you know anything else about her?"

He frowned, trying to remember, then sat bolt upright, hastily grabbing her before she slipped off his lap.

"Sara is the midwife. But you can't... We decided..."

Like all Alliance warriors he'd been given a fertility restrictor, even though he'd told them it was pointless. After they'd settled down on the ranch they'd discussed having it reversed, but he'd been worried that she was too small for childbirth.

"*We* didn't decide. *You* decided," she said, poking his chest. "I was just going to give you a little while to get used to the idea—but you'd better get used to it in the next six months."

"B-but how?"

She shrugged. "Sara said the restrictor is less effective on some species. And you have used your breeding tip several times."

The breeding tip was a wide circle designed to close around his mate's cervix and direct his seed directly to her womb. He knew his cock had assumed that form on several occasions, but he'd never considered that his seed might actually be fertile.

"Six months…" A wave of dizziness washed over him, composed of equal parts joy and terror. "But what if…"

She reached up and put her hand on his face.

"Sara said that I'm perfectly healthy. She doesn't see any reason to be concerned."

A tiny fraction of his fear dissipated as he curved a cautious hand over her stomach.

"She's sure?"

"Yes. And so am I." Her radiant smile also helped. "You'll see—everything is going to be just fine."

He kissed her, his mouth desperate, and she welcomed him as she always did, her fingers buried in his hair.

"A baby," he said when he finally released her.

"Yes. Isn't it wonderful?"

"It's perfect. You're perfect."

His voice was hoarse and she gave him a loving smile.

"Just remember that—and don't think you can spend the next six months babying me."

"Of course not."

She didn't look convinced, shaking her head before kissing him again, and she was right. He spent the next six months doing everything he could to make sure she and the baby were protected. She ignored most of his attempts but gave in often enough that he wasn't completely frantic. Her serene conviction that everything would be all right proved correct.

Six months later she gave birth to the tiniest, most perfect child he could have imagined—a daughter with pale eyes and a tiny tuft of blonde hair—a child he would love and protect for the rest of his life, just as he would her mother.

They named her Melaena, after the female who had first changed his life; the one who had started him on the path to this future.

He was the luckiest male in the world.

THE GRUMPIEST ALIEN ON THE FARM IS UP NEXT! DOES HE also have a part to play in resolving the danger to the farm? Find out in H'zim!

AUTHOR'S NOTE

Thank you so much for reading **Kalpar!** Another cold alien warrior finds love and redemption - and a sweet heroine who is a lot stronger than she seems! I enjoyed dipping my toe into a more romantic suspense vibe with this story, and I hope you liked it!

Whether you enjoyed the story or not, it would mean the world to me if you left an honest review on Amazon – reviews are one of the best ways to help other readers find my books!

As usual, I have to thank my readers for coming on these adventures with me - I couldn't do it without you!

And, as always, a special thanks to my beta team – Janet S, Nancy V, and Kitty S. Your thoughts and comments are incredibly helpful!

How the Aliens Were Won

AUTHOR'S NOTE

continues with **H'zim**

After three years rotting in a jail in Port Cantor, all H'zim wants is to be left alone to lick his wounds and plot his revenge. The last thing he needs is a curvy little human who won't stop talking.

Or maybe she's exactly who he needs…

H'zim is available on Amazon!

And if you'd like to read about more about how the farm became available, check out **You Got Alien Trouble!** - Rosie and Harkan's story!

You Got Alien Trouble! is available on Amazon!

The audio version of **You Got Alien Trouble!** is also available for FREE on my direct store - honeyphillips.myshopify.com!

* * *

To make sure you don't miss out on any new releases, please visit my website and sign up for my newsletter! www.honeyphillips.com

OTHER TITLES

HOMESTEAD WORLDS

Seven Brides for Seven Alien Brothers

Artek

Benjar

Callum

Drakkar

Endark

Frantor

Gilmat

You Got Alien Trouble!

How the Aliens Were Won

Borgaz

Temel

Naffon

S'kal

Celenk

Kalpar

H'zim

Cosmic Fairy Tales

Jackie and the Giant

Blind Date with an Alien
Her Alien Farmhand

Cyborgs on Mars
High Plains Cyborg
The Good, the Bad, and the Cyborg
A Fistful of Cyborg
A Few Cyborgs More
The Magnificent Cyborg
The Outlaw Cyborg
The Cyborg with No Name
Cyborg Rider

KAISARIAN EMPIRE

The Alien Abduction Series
Anna and the Alien
Beth and the Barbarian
Cam and the Conqueror
Deb and the Demon
Ella and the Emperor
Faith and the Fighter
Greta and the Gargoyle

Hanna and the Hitman
Izzie and the Icebeast
Joan and the Juggernaut
Kate and the Kraken
Lily and the Lion
Mary and the Minotaur
Nancy and the Naga
Olivia and the Orc
Pandora and the Prisoner
Quinn and the Queller
Rita and the Raider
Sara and the Spymaster
Tammy and the Traitor

Folsom Planet Blues
Alien Most Wanted: Caged Beast
Alien Most Wanted: Prison Mate
Alien Most Wanted: Mastermind
Alien Most Wanted: Unchained

Stranded with an Alien
Sinta - A SciFi Holiday Tail

Cosmic Cinema
My Fair Alien
The Alien and I

Skruj

Horned Holidays

Krampus and the Crone

A Gift for Nicholas

A Kiss of Frost

Treasured by the Alien

Mama and the Alien Warrior

A Son for the Alien Warrior

Daughter of the Alien Warrior

A Family for the Alien Warrior

The Nanny and the Alien Warrior

A Home for the Alien Warrior

A Gift for the Alien Warrior

A Treasure for the Alien Warrior

Three Babies and the Alien Warrior

Sanctuary for the Alien Warrior

Exposed to the Elements

The Naked Alien

The Bare Essentials

A Nude Attitude

The Buff Beast

The Strip Down

The Alien Invasion Series
Alien Selection
Alien Conquest
Alien Prisoner
Alien Breeder
Alien Alliance
Alien Hope
Alien Castaway
Alien Chief
Alien Ruler

COZY MONSTERS

Fairhaven Falls
Cupcakes for My Orc Enemy
Trouble for My Troll
Fireworks for My Dragon Boss
The Single Mom and the Orc
Mistletoe for My Minotaur
Valentine for My Vampire
Protected by the Orc

Monster Between the Sheets

Extra Virgin Gargoyle
Without a Stitch

Standalones

Hot Wolf in the City
Mated to the Swamp Monster

FANTASY

The Five Kingdoms

The Orc's Hidden Bride
The Orc's Stolen Bride

ABOUT THE AUTHOR

Honey Phillips writes steamy science fiction stories about hot alien warriors and the human women they can't resist. From abductions to invasions, the ride might be rough, but the end always satisfies.

Honey wrote and illustrated her first book at the tender age of five. Her writing has improved since then. Her drawing skills, unfortunately, have not. She loves writing, reading, traveling, cooking, and drinking champagne - not necessarily in that order.

Honey loves to hear from her wonderful readers! You can stalk her at any of the following locations...

www.facebook.com/HoneyPhillipsAuthor
www.bookbub.com/authors/honey-phillips
www.instagram.com/HoneyPhillipsAuthor
www.honeyphillips.com

Printed in Great Britain
by Amazon